THE "FRENCH WRITERS OF
CANADA" SERIES

The purpose of this series is to bring to English readers, for the first time, in a uniform and inexpensive format, a selection of outstanding and representative works by French authors in Canada. Individual titles in the series will range from the most modern work to the classic. Our editors have examined the entire repertory of French fiction in this country to ensure that each book that is selected will reflect important literary and social trends, in addition to having evident aesthetic value.

Current Titles in the Series

Ethel and the Terrorist, a novel by Claude Jasmin, translated by David Walker.

The Temple on the River, a novel by Jacques Hébert, translated by Gerald Taaffe.

Ashini, a novel by Yves Thériault, translated by Gwendolyn Moore.

N'tsuk, a novel by Yves Thériault, translated by Gwendolyn Moore.

The Torrent, novellas and short stories by Anne Hébert, translated by Gwendolyn Moore.

Dr. Cotnoir, a novel by Jacques Ferron, translated by Pierre Cloutier.

Fanny, a novel by Louis Dantin, translated by Raymond Chamberlain.

The Saint Elias, a novel by Jacques Ferron, translated by Pierre Cloutier.

THE "FRENCH WRITERS OF CANADA" SERIES (Continued)

The Juneberry Tree, a novel by Jacques Ferron, translated by Raymond Chamberlain.

Jos Carbone, a novel by Jacques Benoit, translated by Sheila Fischman.

The Grandfathers, a novel by Victor-Lévy Beaulieu, translated by Marc Plourde.

In an Iron Glove, volume one of the autobiography of Claire Martin, translated by Philip Stratford.

The Right Cheek, volume two of the autobiography of Claire Martin, translated by Philip Stratford.

The Forest, a novel by Georges Bugnet, translated by Raymond Chamberlain.

The Poetry of Modern Quebec: an Anthology. edited and translated by Fred Cogswell.

The Brawl, a novel by Gérard Bessette, translated by Marc Lebel and Ronald Sutherland.

Marie Calumet, a novel by Rodolphe Girard, translated by Irène Currie.

Master of the River, a novel by Félix-Antoine Savard, translated by Richard Howard.

Bitter Bread, a novel by Albert Laberge, translated by Conrad Dion.

The Making of Nicolas Montour, a novel by Léo-Paul Desrosiers, translated by Christina Roberts.

(and many more)

Marie Calumet

by
Rodolphe Girard

translated by
Irène Currie

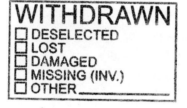

HARVEST HOUSE
Montreal

Advisory Editor
Ben-Zion Shek,
Department of French,
University of Toronto.

Copyright© 1976 by Harvest House Ltd.
First Harvest House edition —
October 1976.
All rights reserved.
Deposited in the Bibliothèque Nationale
of Québec, 4th quarter, 1976.
Originally published by the author
under the title *Marie Calumet,* in 1904.
It was republished in 1973 by Les Editions Fides
with an introduction by Luc Lacourcière.
Copyright © Les Editions Fides — 1973.

For information, address Harvest House Ltd.
4795 St. Catherine St. W., Montreal, H3Z 2B7.

Printed and bound in the United States
Series design by Robert Reid.
Cover illustration: Moe Reinblatt
Cover design: Yair Anavi

Canadian Cataloguing in Publication Data
Girard, Rodolphe, 1879-1956.
[Marie Calumet. English]
Marie Calumet

(The French Writers of Canada series)
Translation of: Marie Calumet.
ISBN paper 88772-1672 (cloth) 88772-230X

I. Title. II. Series.

PS8463.17M313 C843'.5'2 C76-015007-9
PQ3919.G53M313

PREFACE

Long before she became the heroine of a novel, the name of Marie Calumet figured in a folk-song which is deeply ingrained in French-Canadian folklore. Folklorists — those who go to the roots of oral tradition — have collected numerous versions of this song throughout the provinces of Quebec, New Brunswick and even Prince Edward Island. It is a satiric song, following a formula as old as the sixteenth century. Its interior refrain, in fact, provided the framework for a merry song published as early as 1530, in Paris, by Pierre Attaingnant, in his *Musical Songs for Four Voices;* the following are the opening lines in their ancient idiom:

Nous estions troys compaignons
Qui alions de la les monts,
Nous voulions faire grant chere,
Sen devant derrière,
Et sy navions pas ung soulz
Sen dessus dessoubz.

Three great friends are we,
To the hills we flee
Anxious for a feast;
Front and back we go,
If without a sou,
Then back and forth also!

5

In Chapter XI of *De l'Adolescence de Gargantua*, Rabelais also cited this refrain.

Attaingnant's song not only perpetuated itself in popular memory down through the centuries, but its prosodic model has served as a basis for a goodly number of similar songs, "Marie Calumet" among them.

Here then is a literary phenomenon which deserves to be examined briefly on the threshold of the revival of Rodolphe Girard's famous novel. The author must have been aware of the difficulty of his task, for Montreal's *La Presse*, where he worked as a journalist, announced on May 30, 1903, that: "One of our men of letters is at the present time gathering documentation on the famous Marie Calumet who is the subject of a French-Canadian song, but whose history has never been written."

Without embellishment, the song tells of the misadventures that befell a stout girl named Marie Calumet. On the day of her wedding to the priest's hired man, she ate so much stew that she contracted the proverbial runs. The version published by P.E. Prévost, in his *Chansons canadiennes* (1907) chastely limits itself to this initial detail; several other chansonniers digressed even further, laundering it completely in order to achieve easy publication.

Popular tradition, on the other hand, has remained much less prudish. Numerous versions, unpublished to-date but clearly dated and documented, of which the oldest is said to go back as far as 1858 in the Beauce, freely turned "Marie Calumet" into a bawdy song. They embroider the adventure, fleshing out its vicissitudes in more than twenty couplets, of which the following reminds us of the sixteenth century original:

6

Nous étions trois bon garçons
Munis chacun d'un guipon,
Nous la menâmes à la rivière,
Sens dessus dessous, sens devant derrière,
Pour la laver de bout en bout,
Sens devant derrière, sens dessus dessous.

Three fine lads are we
Wielding mops all three;
Took her to the stream,
Front and back we go,
Cleaned her end to end,
Then upside down also!

Girard had reconstituted a composite version of fifteen couplets. But he took great care not to publish it,
nor even to allude to it openly. He merely kept a manu-
script text in his personal copy of the novel and gave
copies to his friends, E.Z. Massicotte and Albert
Laberge, who had helped him with his research. It is not
certain that together they did not add figments of their
own invention to the text. Only a comparative study of
all the fragments extant could throw light on the matter.

However this may be, the first question which comes
to mind is this: What does the novel owe to the song?
Both all and almost nothing, depending on the point of
view the reader takes. Apart from its title, it is first of all
the framework of an adventure: a wedding feast in a
rectory. Onto this sparse canvas the novelist embroiders
an entire intrigue, which he situates in the fictitious
parish of Saint Ildefonse* in the region of Nicolet. His

---

* Girard's village names are nearly all satirical. *Ildefonse*, for
example, translates as "he destroys" or "he breaks up"; *Saint Apollinaire* is a real saint, but also recalls the Greek god, as well as
Guillaume Apollinaire, the avant-garde French poet and critic whose
defense of Cubism was current when *Marie Calumet* was written.

protagonists, of course, are the opulent housekeeper, Marie Calumet, "who is marching on forty," Curé Flavel, a good-natured priest, and Narcisse Boisvert, his hired man, who is as shy with his fellow humans as he is diligent in his work. They are surrounded by the contrasting characters of Suzon, the priest's niece in the splendor of her seventeen years, Curé Lefranc, a neighboring priest with liberal ideas, and Zéphirin, a verger of vindictive temperament. But I do not intend to give a synopsis of the novel here. Suffice it to say that it ends approximately where the song begins and consists of about twenty tableaux of humorous realism, enhanced by a cheerful style which today appears to us to be entirely inoffensive.

In 1904, however, it was looked upon otherwise. In the romantic climate of that intolerant epoch, *Marie Calumet* was condemned as an abominable crime. It caused indignant outcries from all quarters. The weekly *La Semaine Religieuse* denounced the novel as immoral and ungodly. *La Presse* disowned its author and brutally fired him. At the age of twenty-five, Rodolphe Girard was forced to seek refuge in Ottawa where he continued to be harassed. Witness the defamatory libel suit he instituted in 1908 against *La Vérité* in Quebec, an action which did not end in his favor until 1911 in the Superior Court and Court of Appeals.

Girard published other novels, as well as collections of short stories and novellas, both before and after 1904. Several of his plays were produced but nothing succeeded in his obtaining forgiveness for *Marie Calumet*. Critics in general showed themselves neither generous nor indulgent towards his work. Certainly his novel did not lack flaws; but it was not always these that were seen in the condemnation of his work. Perhaps there was not enough material for a novel of this length; a few pages are irrelevant to the book or less than well integrated into its action. But sixty years after its publication, the work appears to us under a very different light: it is a joyous documentary on country mores of days gone by. And it is one of the rare novels of the era which retains a certain freshness in its easy grace. On that count alone, we have not hesitated to reserve it a place among Canadian works to be reread. Here then is Rodolphe Girard's revenge, accomplished without the help of "Leaden Wood."

LUC LACOURCIÈRE

MARIE CALUMET

Marie Calumet va se marier, (bis)
Avec le garçon de Monsieur le curé, (bis)
Les noces se font au presbytère,
Sens dessus dessous, sens devant derrière,
Nous y sommes invités tous,
Sens devant derrière, sens dessus dessous.

Nous avions un bon repas, (bis)
Muni de bons pâtés fort gras, (bis)
D'un ragoût et des tourtières,
Sens dessus dessous, sens devant derrière,
Nous en avons mangé tous,
Sens devant derrière, sens dessus dessous.

Le lendemain elle s'en est allée (bis)
Avec son mari pour demeurer. (bis)
Comme elle était bonne cuisinière,
Sens dessus dessous, sens devant derrière,
Elle lui fit du bon ragoût,
Sens devant derrière, sens dessus dessous.

Ils en ont, tous deux, tant mangé, (bis)
Qu'ils eurent à la fois le corps dérangé. (bis)
Son mari lui dit: "Je compte ben, ma chère,"
Sens dessus dessous, sens devant derrière,
"Q'tas mis trop d'épices dans ton ragoût,"
Sens devant derrière, sens dessus dessous.

MARIE CALUMET

Marie Calumet will be wed today *(bis)*
To the hired man of M'sieu l'curé *(bis)*
Into the home of the good priest,
Front and back we go
Invites us all to feast,
Then back and forth also!

All we did was eat 'til we could hold no more, *(bis)*
Tasted rich patés and tourtières galore, *(bis)*
And every kind of pie and stew
Front and back we go
Full to the brim anew
Then back and forth also!

When the feast was over, she waved good-bye, *(bis)*
Followed her new husband to his house nearby. *(bis)*
The finest cook we ever knew,
Front and back we go
She often served him dainty ragout.
Then back and forth also!

One fine day they ate so much of her ragout *(bis)*
That they both were stricken with the stomach flu. *(bis)*
Her husband groaned, "Oh dear! Oh dear!"
Front and back we go
"This stew is over-spiced, I fear!"
Then back and forth also!

ACKNOWLEDGMENTS

For the best of reasons, we have retained the excellent preface by Luc Lacourcière to the Fides French-language edition of 1973. We are indebted to John Robert Colombo for the English translation of the verse which appears in the "Preface" and Chapter XV of this edition.

The song "Marie Calumet" which appears in the preliminary pages of this book is taken from Paul-Emile Prévost, *Chansons canadiennes, paroles et musique par nos canadiens,* harmonisées par P.-E. Prévost, Montreal, 1907.

The Publishers gratefully acknowledge a translation grant from The Canada Council.

Chapter I

The Two Priests

On that evening, Monsieur le curé of Saint Ildefonse had asked his neighbor, the influential pastor of the wealthy parish of Saint Apollinaire, to stay for supper.

Curé Flavel was not rich, but — by Jove — when you ask a friend to break bread with you, it matters little that you belong to the good Lord's establishment and are not accustomed to revelling at Sardanapalian feasts! You still would not ask for His blessing or say grace over a few lowly crusts!

And so, the good Monsieur le curé Flavel, well-bred and hospitable man that he was, had graciously gone to some expense. Not as great, mind you, as would have been warranted by a visit from the deputy of the county nor, certainly, by the bishop of the diocese.

The curé of Saint Apollinaire was enthusiastically addicted to the pleasures of the table; he was never more affable with his parishioners than at the threshold of a dining room. Now, as hot and pungent aromas emanated from the kitchen — they seemed to be impregnating every piece of furniture in the rectory — Monsieur le curé Lefranc's nostrils began to quiver and, having demurred briefly for the sake of convention, he gratefully accepted the invitation.

Half an hour later, they entered the dining room. It was a room which resembled all others of its kind. In its center stood a rectangular table; in a corner, a sideboard. There were chairs with seats of woven straw, their backs carelessly daubed with yellow paint; a few house plants; a rag carpet made by some local artisan. On the walls, covered with cheap wallpaper, hung a worthless colored lithograph: "Joseph Sold by his Brothers." Another picture, speckled with flydirt, represented "Jesus Among the Physicians." In the far corner, a few family portraits; and in the place of honor, the center of the main wall, a large black crucifix on which a plaster Christ, hands and feet bloodstained, was impaled.

The meal consisted of cabbage soup (left over from lunch), roast beef with gravy, breast of veal with peas, rabbit stew, butter, pickles, radishes, coffee with milk, and dessert. Before they began to eat, Curé Flavel and his friend turned towards the crucifix and prayed. *"Benedicite, Domine, nos et ea quae sumus sumpturi benedicat dextera Christi."*

The pastor of Saint Ildefonse only picked at his food; his friend, on the other hand, attacked it with gusto. Not that the food merited a blue ribbon. Certainly not. The soup was like mortar — anyone trying to brave it ran the risk of having his intestines fused into a solid mass. The roast was tough as leather because it had been cooked so long; the veal so rare that the poor animal might well have just expired under the carving knife; the rabbit stew salty as seaweed.

When they were ready for dessert, Curé Flavel called, "Suzon!"

An adorable child of seventeen at most, with a sunny smile and a forehead shaded by stray, ash-blond curls, thrust her head through the half-open door which con-

14

nected the kitchen to the dining room. A hint of irony deliciously raised the corners of her mouth, creating two seductive dimples on her cheeks, which the overheated kitchen had set on fire.

"Monsieur le curé called?" she asked.

"Bring us the strawberry tarts and some honey. Not the brown, but the good white honey I harvested myself last week and had my ear stung for it into the bargain."

The young woman was about to return to the kitchen.

"Just a moment," added Curé Flavel. "Haven't I told you a hundred times to leave off the formality? Why is it that you always address me as 'Monsieur le curé?' Why, when I'm in my chancel and turn towards the faithful and say 'My dearest brothers,' I'm not as formal as you are. Simply call me 'uncle.' That would be so much easier... and more respectful, too."

Opening the door more fully, Suzon advanced a few paces. She approached the table, where the last rays of the setting sun accentuated her youthful beauty. The priest from Saint Apollinaire regarded her calmly and appreciatively.

Like a schoolgirl caught perpetrating some mischief and scolded by her Mother Superior, the pretty child stared chastely at the tips of her shoes which imprisoned a pair of tiny feet. Curé Lefranc openly admired a delicate ankle, guessing at a well-turned calf and, further, at matchless legs losing themselves in the folds of her skirt, which was blue calico printed with daisies as white and pure as the soul of the child. Her rounded hips, slender waist, and fluttering breast — which gave only a hint of its firm blooming — would have stirred a less austere man.

Dutifully, he directed his thoughts to heaven, being

careful, however, not to take his eyes off the ground.

"Very well, uncle," said Suzon, raising a rakish eye. "There's more to come. We also have custard, floating island, melon, apples, plum jam, cheese, and rhubarb wine. The good rhubarb wine, y'know, the one you swill a large tumblerful of every night before you go to bed at nine."

"Come now, you talk too much, my daughter. As with all your sisters, the good Lord forgot to cut off a piece of your tongue."

"Which you could probably use in some of your sermons, Monsieur le curé."

And with the lightness of a lark's wing, the young imp fled, leaving the room filled with the sound of her clear laughter. The old furniture of the rectory seemed to be hopping with indignation.

What could Curé Flavel do but shrug his shoulders and shake his head?

His colleague, on the other hand, was frankly enchanted. "Believe me, my friend, your niece is a jewel…"

He stopped short. Suzon had just returned with the dessert. She glanced at her uncle, affecting a contrite and repentant countenance whenever he looked her way.

Retreating to the kitchen once again, she asked, "Will there be anything else, uncle?"

"No, thank you. Only do not forget to milk the cow. And take a pint of milk to Marcelline, whose poor husband we buried last Tuesday."

When the young woman had gone, Curé Flavel passed the plum jam to the pastor of Saint Apollinaire. "My friend," he scolded, "these words from your mouth surprise me profoundly and, I must admit, such profane admiration affects me similarly. How can a

16

man, ordained to be a priest by the will of God, take pleasure in a pretty face! Look at me! I can tell you in all honesty that in the twenty years I have been serving this parish, I have yet to notice which of my faithful are pretty and which aren't.''

''That's because you lack a sense of aesthetics,'' retorted Curé Lefranc, nibbling on a plum pit.

Curé Flavel was nevertheless speaking the truth. He was born to the priesthood as others are born to be laborers, physicians, blacksmiths, notaries, wheelwrights, vergers, or bailiffs. His fiftieth birthday had come and gone. When he had been a young lad, his father and mother, worthy farmers from Gentilly, had held a family council and there his future had been decided.

''We'll make our Jacques a priest. Folks will respect us when they say: 'The son of Eustache Flavel is a priest!' '' And when his good wife remarked that to become a Monsieur le curé one had to have a classical education and that a classical education cost pennies — four years, in fact, of good harvests, provided the soil produced well — the head of the family had overruled her objections. ''Don't worry your head, woman, don't lose sleep over such trifles. Zacharie's boy, now, he's going to school, and Zacharie and his wife are as poor as we are. I've even heard it said that they're hard put keeping the wolf from the door. Now, M'sieu le notaire studied in Montreal, and he tells me there's priests there, Sulpicians they call themselves, rich ones, good and rich, and they're s'posed to be helping out young folk that wants to take the cloth. All we have to do is tell them that our Jacques wants to take holy orders and I'll bet you two to one those Sulpicians will give him a bursary. A bursary, from what the notary tells me, that's reduction of at least forty bucks a year.

17

So if we cut down on our expenses, we might just find a way to send him there. Leave it to me, woman, 'cause Eustache Flavel will take care of everything.''

And Eustache Flavel had taken such good care of everything that Jacques went away to school, failed his baccalaureat, and, in good time, came to take holy orders. It goes without saying that our worthy seminarian never ventured to see even a little of the world; he might have risked losing his vocation. His village, the long corridors of the seminary — which some rascals dared to compare to the Mamertine Jail — and the more deserted streets of Montreal where young seminarians and the clergy took their walks on their days off — that was the sum of his experience.

In appearance, the pastor of Saint Ildefonse was a man of modest height, tending to portliness. His graying hair was becoming sparse at the top of his head and his florid face, always freshly shaven, was reminiscent of a full moon. Rarely out of sorts, he was by temperament as gentle as a lamb, and his devotion to his dear Lord, his flock, and his bees was boundless. Did he have any faults? None at all. Small imperfections at most. For example, a greatly marked predilection for his rhubarb wine and for the excellent Canadian tobacco harvested from his own soil.

The pastor of Saint Apollinaire, by contrast, was wont to display the rather liberal ideas which gave his neighbor such cause for worry and discontent. At his Jesuit college, his spiritual director had forcefully assured him that he had the calling. This, however, the young man had wished to put to the test himself. And so it was that, on the completion of his studies, he had wandered off a little in every direction, to the left, to the right, here lifting the veil partially, there pushing it aside altogether. Two years later he had returned, begging humbly, "Bless me, father, I have sinned. Accept me into your ranks, for I do have the calling."

"Even so shall there be joy in heaven over one sinner that repenteth, rather than over ninety-nine just who have no need of repentance."

Chapter II

"To Each His Own Métier and The Cows Won't Go Astray"

Monsieur le curé Lefranc had begun his ministry as a humble assistant in a parish of Nicolet County. After a time, he was able to use certain influences with the bishop of the diocese and was promptly put in charge of the parish of Saint Apollinaire. Of his youthful passions he had retained only his love of horses. He was a fanatic horsedealer and owner of a prize mare whose trotting time was a respectable 2:18, a detail which, innocent as it may seem, earned him considerable respect among his parishioners. It was not surprising, then, that his mildly audacious remarks had shocked Curé Flavel; indeed, it would have taken less to unsettle the saintly man who was already beginning to swell with righteous anger.

"Ah yes," said Curé Flavel, filling his friend's glass with rhubarb wine, "you have traveled much, seen much, learned much. You may well indulge in fancy talk whereas I, my God... I don't know a great deal. The sum of my wisdom is confined to my theological dissertation on Saint Thomas, my Bible and my breviary. But I am content with what little I know, for my parishioners appear to be satisfied with my ministry. Last week, for instance, you were discussing politics and social problems, none of which I understand. Why do you insist on bending my ear with highfaluting words that are all too often devoid of meaning? The whole lot of politicians, with their ideas and shenanigans, don't interest me as much as the overturned plow you see there on the far side of the road. A good country priest like me should not concern himself with politics. And even if he did, he should keep his convictions and opinions to himself. You know as well as I that a priest's task is to guide and save the souls entrusted to his care. It's not for him to alienate people's spirits by supporting and promoting a political party, whatever it is.''

Curé Flavel was beginning to work himself into a state. He rose from the table and, preceding his friend to the study, began to stuff his pipe.

Curé Lefranc availed himself of this opportunity to parry. ''Go on with you! What an old twaddler you are! Backward spirit! Crusty shaveling! Since when does a free man, be he a Christian minister, a Muslim imam or a Buddhist monk, no longer have the right to form opinions on public affairs and to express them if he so desires?''

''Easy now, my friend,'' Curé Flavel retorted. ''Would you like to know why you are facing a mountain of difficulties with some of your faithful who give you so much trouble that you no longer know which saint to pray to? I'll tell you why and I'll make no bones about it. It's because you stick your nose into what's none of your business. You know very well that our people are by nature spiteful and suspicious. Therefore, if a country priest steps out of bounds, he will provoke chills and inspire resentments for which he must pay dearly when it comes to carrying out the duties of his ministry.''

"And I say that it's up to us to enlighten our flocks so that they may vote according to their consciences. Whose task is that, pray tell, if not the curé's?"

"Bah! There you go again with your fancy words. They remind me of the empty drum I keep behind my kitchen door. Give it a good kick and it will produce all manner of noise. My dear friend, you have stirred the consciences of your parishioners so well that you have made yourself an army of enemies. To each his own métier and the cows won't go astray, I always say."

Curé Flavel had taken good aim. His arrow hit its mark. His friend sat chewing his lip. To help him regain his composure, he stared fixedly at his accuser and opened fire. "And what about you? For a straight-laced fellow with such lofty morals, you're a fine one to talk! It's you who should worry about people! One does not, after all, house such a charming girl under the roof of a rectory with impunity. Such a beautiful child... and if..."

"She's my niece, for heaven's sake!"

"Niece, indeed! You know perfectly well that sins are committed between uncles and nieces, between sisters-in-law and brothers-in-law! All I'm saying is that the opportunity is there. Mind you, personally, I don't object to your niece's living here; every priest raises one. Nieces are like pretty pieces of furniture and belong in every rectory. The trouble is that it isn't proper."

"And," he added, pointing a threatening finger at his colleague, "whoever exposes himself to danger will perish in it!"

At first, Suzon's uncle thought that his friend was only joking. When he realized that Curé Lefranc was quite serious, he began to look as guilty as a little child whose mother has just surprised him dipping a wet finger into the sugar bowl.

"Well... perhaps you have something there. It would never have occurred to me. Still, people are so mean and so fond of gossip. Ever since old Marianne left the rectory, everything has gone wrong, everything's in a dreadful mess. I had hoped that perhaps my niece could become a good housekeeper, but at the moment, she's young, she's full of mischief, she's empty headed. How do you expect me to keep things running smoothly with that sort of a girl? You know, I've never been lucky with housekeepers. So far, I've not found one who has suited me."

"That's not surprising, considering how little you know about women. But wait... yes, that's it! I know one... and she would be exactly the kind of woman you need."

"She mustn't be too young, mind. The bishop doesn't like our housekeepers to be blooming. Personally, I wouldn't care, but there's no arguing with his rules."

"Rest assured. Would I let you get your paws on a pretty girl who isn't even your niece?" Curé Lefranc said, winking at his friend.

To contain his indignation, Curé Flavel, who was now close to apoplexy, blew his nose into an enormous blue and white-checked handkerchief. "On the other hand," said the saintly man, "it wouldn't do to hire one so old that she can't get out of bed thirty-nine days out of forty."

"Put your mind at rest. The woman I will be sending you will do for your establishment what the late M'sieu Joseph did for the kingdom of Egypt."

Smiling with anticipation, like some poor devil sampling a life of future delights, Curé Flavel rubbed his hands. "My dear friend. If only I could find the perfect housekeeper. What bliss! No longer would I eat those awful pebbly tarts or potatoes that are welded to the bottom of the saucepan three hundred and sixty times a year. No more coffee resembling dishwater or peppers that set my mouth on fire. My house would be…"

"Enough, my friend, enough. I fear that you are about to launch into an entire litany of jeremiads, and I warn you, I do not care for complainers. I had better say good night and good luck."

"Don't walk away like a savage, in the middle of the evening! Here, let me pour you another drop of my rhubarb wine. Just look at it! Clear as spring water. And how it sparkles!" And Curé Flavel sipped his brew, sniffing its bouquet and clicking his tongue. His friend nodded approval.

They were silent.

"I would consider it a favor," suddenly begged the master of the house, "if you would stay with me for the rest of the evening. We could play a game of cards, smoke together, and you could spend the night under my roof."

"And what about my Mass?"

"You could leave early. The roads are good, you have a fine horse. It won't take long to travel the two miles."

"Done!"

At eleven o'clock, Curé Flavel, carrying a lamp — the advent of gas and electricity being too recent to have reached the village of Saint Ildefonse — led his friend to the guest-room.

At that moment, Monsieur le curé's niece, for reasons of her own, left her small chamber. She was wearing a nightgown, and her hair hung down her back

24

in a long braid. When she reached the landing, she suddenly found herself in the presence of the two men. With a small cry of distress, she scampered off like a doe, her hand modestly covering the opening left by the unbuttoned collar of her yellow nightgown.

To overcome his acute embarrassment, Curé Flavel cleared his throat.

His friend, on the other hand, was jubilant. "Ah, Saint Antoine," he exclaimed, balling his fists, "how could you have withstood so many onslaughts, if all those women who tempted you were like this one?"

He opened the door to the room in which he was to spend the night and recoiled. "Is this where I sleep?"

The master of the house could hardly be flattered by the expression on his friend's face.

Let the reader imagine the room of a commercial traveler in which the occupant has just scattered all his samples. A veritable catch-all, where a cow would have been unable to locate her calf.

"Well, good night."

"Good night."

They shook hands warmly.

"Did you sleep well, at least?" Monsieur le curé Flavel asked his friend the next morning, as the latter prepared to climb into his carrriage.

"Don't remind me of it! My ribs could not be more bruised if I had slept on a clothesline. Why, even a Carthusian monk would have shunned your wretched cot. Ah, my poor friend, you are indeed in urgent need of a housekeeper. If you don't find one soon, you'll be ruined! Ruined!"

Chapter III

Desolation at the Rectory

Despite his sunny disposition, Monsieur le curé Flavel, who was only human, had his bad days. And on such days he was indeed a sad sight! Not that his gloominess showed itself in any way like the brusque moods of his friend. No, for him it was as though a heavy burden had been placed on his shoulders, and sometimes, without quite knowing why, he would discover a large tear in the corner of his eye.

This was unquestionably out of character for the kindly country curé, who had never known himself to have the slightest leaning towards sentimentality.

On the morning in question Monsieur le curé had, as the saying goes in our part of the country, "got out of bed with his heavy end first."

The weight of the entire world seemed to be pressing down on the dear man's heart. All night long, he had been plagued by the most dreadful nightmares: Marius weeping over the ruins of Carthage, devastation in the Holy City, the coming of Judgment Day. Already bathed in sweat and filled with horror, he had suddenly seen the fieldstone walls of his rectory contract — contract until he felt that his very bones were about to be crushed. Trembling on its foundation, the church itself was threatened with ruin. Its tin-plate spire, already rusted with rain and age, began to crumble; the rectory, the church, the entire village teetered on the brink of collapse. It was at this precise moment that the figure of a woman had appeared in the clouds.

Seated on a humble cart with the majestic bearing of a goddess in her blazing chariot, she had floated slowly to earth, proffering a helping hand to the desperate priest. Boundless relief had immediately flooded the heart of the stricken man. The walls began to recede, the belltower lifted its head once again, and the houses returned to their foundations. A shimmering halo surrounded the rectory. It was salvation.

Curé Flavel awoke in a state of extreme exhaustion, feeling like Jacob after his battle with the angel. The uninterrupted succession of nightmares had flung him into a state of prostration from which he had not yet recovered. Most of all, he was affected by the imminent ruin of his rectory. And what was the tearful Marius doing in his dreams? His college days held no memories to foster such excruciating nightmares. And what about the devastation in the Holy City, the foundering of his parish. It must have been a warning from above. A great calamity was going to befall him. A great calamity? But no, there could be no great calamity befalling Monsieur le curé Flavel, for had not a woman appeared in the sky to save him and his flock? Dear God! What a feeling! What a feeling!

The bell, calling the villagers to Low Mass, began to ring just as he was putting the finishing touches to his rather neglected appearance. He took his hat and went out. The handful of people who had come to attend the service awaited him. Awkwardly, they raised their large straw hats as the priest passed. He returned their greetings with a fatherly nod. He had just begun the

Mass when the young altar boy, arms swinging, came clip-clopping through the church in his heavy cowhide boots.

Not even the holy Mass succeeded in banishing the haunting and lugubrious preoccupations from the consciousness of the saintly curé. For a man in his lofty position, he found himself guilty of unforgivable absent-mindedness indeed! He would have read the Gospel before the Gradual, had not his young altar boy, who, it must be said, was no dumbbell, saved the day by very humbly tugging at his alb. But there was worse to come. A few minutes later, he turned towards the faithful and, instead of wishing them the peace of Christ, *"Dominus Vobiscum,"* he told them roundly and in a fairly loud voice that it was time to go home, *"Ite missa est!"*

For the first time in her life, the village spinster, Josette, a wise old woman whose dress and figure had seen better days, raised her eyes to her vicar. Josette, who had never once missed Low Mass since being struck from the list of "marrying girls," finally had something to confess.

"What's come over our curé today?" the faithful wondered as they were leaving the church. "He's never had such lapses, never! Something is bound to happen to us soon, for sure!"

From mere conjecture, they went on to certainty. In less than an hour the entire village was talking in hushed voices. "Y'know, Monsieur le curé's hiding something from us. Something big's going to happen, for sure!"

After breakfast, prepared by himself — his niece having elected to linger in the warmth of her bed — and consisting of gruel smothered in cream, a slice of salt pork, two boiled eggs, a spoonful of honey, and coffee made of roast barley, Monsieur le curé stuffed his meerschaum pipe. All our priests, besides a niece, are proud possessors of a meerschaum pipe.

Hands thrust into the pockets of his trousers (through openings cut especially into his cassock), Monsieur le curé started pacing restlessly up and down his porch. Finally, he went out into his garden which was situated between the rectory and the gravel sidewalk.

The poor little garden had seen better days. Geraniums, their sparse petals battered, sadly bent their heads; no longer velvet-soft and fresh as dewdrops, the pansies thought only of dying; the sweet peas, at the foot of the barbed-wire fence, had lost their delicate perfume; pale and sun-parched, four or five carnations looked at each other with heavy hearts and sighed, like Trappists, "Brothers, it is time to die." A few steps along the way, the blossoms of the snowball tree were no longer of this world; the fragrant mignonette had just gone to its reward, its head falling sadly over its stem; the elegant hyacinth was doing penance for its former glory. And all along the path, the wild cucumbers raised their shriveled arms to heaven and begged for mercy.

Moved to tears, Monsieur le curé Flavel walked towards the poultry yard. Here, too, desolation held sway. His hens were pecking listlessly, sadly rolling their round, gold-speckled eyes. Even the rooster had forgotten his former ardor and ignored his loved ones. The turkey gobbled mournfully, and, in the nearby field, the cows intoned a cacophonic choir which might have been entitled "Funeral March for an Entire Poultry Yard."

Pursuing his sorrowful journey, the priest now came to the whitewashed dairy shed, only to find it in the same sad state of abandonment. Basins and pails were scattered everywhere. A saucerful of honey floated in a bowl of milk. A sheaf of garlic had fallen into a cream-filled soup plate. Fifine, the rectory's wily black cat, had slipped through a door, which had been carelessly left ajar, and was filling her belly more assiduously than ever. The rascal had just disposed of a dish of milk and, resting now, was licking her bedewed chops and whiskers with her small pink tongue.

"Out with you!" shouted her master and made ready to strike the animal. But Fifine, true to her feline nature, sensed danger and shot away like an arrow, her whiskers brushing against the pastor's cassock in passing.

Uttering a fathomless sigh, Monsieur le curé returned to the house, entering the kitchen by way of the vestibule. The massive cast-iron stove was encrusted with layers of rust, grease, and dust. Dirty dishes not only filled the sink to overflowing but also littered the oilcloth-covered table.

Cauldrons, saucepans, pots, bowls, kettles, teapots, coffeepots, dripping pans, and glasses were everywhere. Under the table, the household dog, an exceedingly filthy spaniel, was defending his meager morsel against Fifine who, with arching back and bristling tail, was seeking revenge for the humiliation suffered in the milk shed. In the center of the kitchen, its four legs jutting upwards, a chair sprawled pitifully on the dirty, mud-caked floor. Passing through the dining room, the pastor went into his study. Every piece of furniture was covered with dust. The cretonne curtains hung limp as funeral crepe; the ribbons used to tie them to the wall were in shreds.

Opening his account books, Monsieur le curé was shocked to discover the state of his affairs. The year's budget, with such laughable figures as these, would be a disaster, no matter what amounts he would be able to collect in tithes.

Chapter IV

"My Apparition!"

On June 28, 1860, Marie Calumet made her triumphant entrance into the village of Saint Ildefonse. On that day, the villagers, already bewildered by the strange behavior of their curé, were on the alert.

They could feel it in their bones — an extraordinary event was about to take place.

Saint Ildefonse is built along a single road, one end of which plunges into the Saint Lawrence River and the other, having wended its way over an area of five or six miles, is attached to a bridge. Beyond the small river it spans lies the next parish, the domain of Monsieur le curé Lefranc.

On one side, the river's silvery reflections can be seen gleaming in the sunlight which filters through the thick, green branches of elm, walnut, oak, birch, and maple trees, all growing helter-skelter, arms entwined like good friends albeit of different races. On the other side lies the daily bread of the farms: fields of hay, wheat, oats, barley, and buckwheat. A little further on rises a hillock which the traveler to Saint Apollinaire must bypass and from whose summit the belltower of Saint Ildefonse can be seen pointing into the sky.

Nine o'clock. A morning to inspire an artist. The breath of heat and labor was rising into a misty blue sky dotted with a few whispy clouds. Everyone was hard at work.

Pulled by a pair of powerful draught horses, a mower was just disappearing into the hollow of a valley. A lad with a pair of iron fists and a robust wench, arms bare to her sunburned elbows, were building haycocks, gaily singing *"Par derrière chez ma tante."* Two small lads had climbed onto a heavily laden wagon and were tumbling in the hay, pulling each other's hair and turning somersaults, while an elderly but still vigorous farmer was straining a little to thrust up more huge bundles of hay from the end of his gleaming pitchfork. In the next field, startled by the sound of shrill commands, his chubby flanks stung by the whip, a thick-rumped, mottled-gray Percheron climbed the hill on stiff legs and made for the barn whose double-winged door stood wide open. And everywhere, in the ditches and in the hollows, wallowing in the juicy grass, squabbled swarms of playful little urchins.

In the midst of all this life, the sun rose, leaden. And with it rose the dust from the road, the chirp of the crickets from the hay, and the blackbirds' song from the cherry and apple trees. Sparrows perched in broken rows on telegraph lines. A fieldmouse scurried across the rocks until it was nailed to the ground by a tedder's pitchfork.

No vehicle ever passes unnoticed in our part of the country. All eyes turn in its direction, faces are pressed against windowpanes, and front porches become overt observation posts. That goes for ordinary occurrences. But on June 28, 1860, it was more than that. It was a sensation!

The first thing our folk saw was the outline of a tired nag as it appeared in the distance at the point where the road makes a sharp turn. Now, a cart hove into view, laden with countless bundles of clothing, cardboard boxes, and a portemanteau decorated with vividly colored flowers — in short, an entire moving train on top of which, beside a young villager, a woman sat majestically enthroned. The animal seemed to be aware of the status and importance of its charge, for it advanced with a gleam of pride in its large wall-eyes.

To obtain a better view, our countryfolk craned their necks and shouted, "Ouf. Now what might that be?"

"D'you know her?"

"No. You?"

"Not me!"

The mare stopped in mid-road for reasons which, once upon a time, had caused Bucephalus to act in like manner.

"Dirty animal!" protested the woman, turning crimson with embarrassment.

"Go on with you! Forward!" shouted the carter, lashing the mare's ribs with a long cane.

Now the cart entered the village. Never, in living memory, had anything, not even the archbishop's carriage, impressed the people of Saint Ildefonse as profoundly as this mysterious equipage. And when it came to a halt across the street from the rectory and they had to admit that they were not dreaming, their mouths dropped in amazement and shock. It was all a mistake, for sure!

Women stepped out of their houses, carrying babies in their arms. Toddlers clung to their skirts.

Monsieur le curé Flavel, at that moment, was reading his breviary with his usual devotion. Under his large black straw hat, he was pacing his garden with small steps, causing the gravel to squeek beneath his feet.

"Whoah!"

The priest raised his eyes and turned pale. The book fell to his feet. "My apparition!" he murmured.

Like a refreshing dew, the memory of the dream of that very night — oh, happy coincidence — brought ineffable consolation to his bruised soul. Monsieur le curé's entire household — the hired man, the verger, and Suzon — now assembled. All three, animated by different feelings, surrounded their pastor like a noble guard to receive the newcomer with all the honors due to her station.

Curé Flavel waited with ill-concealed emotion.

Narcisse, the hired man, blurted out, "A creature!" And leaped forward. For one instant, he held the "creature" between heaven and earth. Slowly, he lowered her to the ground like a flower of which one must take good care so as not to break the stem.

Their eyes met, and in that moment a romance, fraught with fateful consequences, was born. Tears and anger, laughter and happiness were to be its outcome.

"I thank you," she said.

"T'was nothing," said Monsieur le curé's hired man, struck to the heart.

All eyes riveted on her, the newcomer now advanced, straight as a ramrod, towards the priest who could not help feeling troubled by all this attention, all this staring, all this intense scrutiny.

"Good day, M'sieu le curé," said the lady with self-assurance and a slight inclination of her head.

She opened her handbag and withdrew from it a letter which she handed to Curé Flavel. In a low voice, but audible to everyone present, he read:

My dear friend,

> With this letter I introduce you to Mlle.
> Marie Calumet. She is a good and worthy
> woman, and a housekeeper without peer.
> She has no vices and can provide you with
> any reference you may need, starting with
> mine.

> Keep well,

> J. Lefranc, priest.

"Are you Mademoiselle Marie Calumet?" asked Curé
Flavel.

"Yes, M'sieu le curé, at your service."

"Well then, make yourself at home. Come in for a
rest and a bite to eat. The trip must have made you
hungry."

"And you, too," he added, turning towards the man
who had accompanied Marie Calumet.

"Oh, thank you, M'sieu le curé. If I weren't in such
a rush to take my whey to the dairy..."

"A drop of rhubarb wine, at least," insisted the
pastor.

"That I can't refuse," answered the man, stammer-
ing with timidity.

They went into the dining room of the rectory.
Aided by Suzon, Marie Calumet took off a black straw
bonnet, which was trimmed with lemon-yellow and
blood-red flowers. This creation had been fastened
under its wearer's chin with large ribbons of whitish
satinette. With elaborate precaution, Marie Calumet
now placed her saffron-yellow wool shawl, printed
with arabesques and trimmed with a fringe border, on a
chair which she took care to dust beforehand with her
fingertips. She wore this garment year-round — in the

suffocating heat of July as well as during the glacial cold of February.

A small, silver-plated cross, suspended around her neck on a puce-colored ribbon, completed her outfit. She valued this piece of jewelry as highly as she valued her eyes.

Marie Calumet, to use her own expression, was marching on forty. When she had entered upon the thirty-ninth year of her life, she was marching on forty and today, eleven months and twenty-nine days later, she still marched on forty. With each birthday, the game began anew. Marie Calumet was forever marching; only death would stop her.

It cannot be said that she was a beautiful woman. No, rather she was a comely "creature," as the people of Sainte Geneviève, where she had seen the light of day, would have it. And yet, whoever, once in his life, laid eyes on Marie Calumet would never forget her again. Tall, with a stately figure and even more stately bust, she overflowed with health and fat. Her ebony-black hair, parted impeccably and smoothed into shiny strands, was pulled back to her neck, there to form an imposing chignon into which she had inserted a penny-store comb.

Need it be added that her skin was very white, her cheeks as red and smooth as a prize apple, because her life, thus far, had been so peaceful, so serene? There was not a cloud in her sky, not a wrinkle on her brow. A few cranks, it is true, judged her nose to be too turned up, her mouth a little large. But not even the tiny tufts of hair nestling in the dimple of her chin detracted in any way from the rustic grace of Marie Calumet. So much for her physique.

As to her moral attributes, Monsieur le curé Flavel's

new servant had a heart of gold coupled with a forceful nature. On the autumn morning of her mother's death, she had vowed not to desert her widowed old father. That is why she, the eldest of the family, had never married. She had taken her mother's place with the little ones, bathing, scrubbing, dressing and wiping them as clean as she could. Now, the girls had found themselves "marrying men," the boys were settled, the old man had just died, and Marie found herself at loose ends. That was what Curé Lefranc had in mind when he recommended the old maid to his neighbor.

To complete this rapid sketch, I will admit that Marie Calumet was not without her idiosyncrasies — among others, a passion for color and eccentric clothes. Also, she was touchingly, childishly naive and not a little gullible. All matters pertaining to religion inspired her with exaggerated admiration and awe which she could now project onto the august person of Monsieur le curé. Yes, she was fond of giving orders, but once someone became the object of her devotion, it was forever. She carried devotion to such extremes that its objects would, in the end, become part of her, even belong to her.

Thus, on the day of her arrival, she said, "I'll be off now to milk Monsieur le curé's cows." The next day she improved on this, "Our cows give us a lot of milk, for sure." And by the third day, looking tenderly at the animals grazing within the confines of the rectory field, she would remark, "Those dear cows of mine sure need a lot of good care."

Does the reader now perceive what a treasure Monsieur le curé had just acquired? He must have, indeed, especially if he has guessed that Marie Calumet, despite some of her striking characteristics, had a flair for the practical things of life — the very things of which, as we have seen, the pastor's bible and theology had taught him nothing.

Chapter V

"Gracious Sainte Anne!
Did You Ever See Such a Mess?"

"Gracious Sainte Anne! Did you ever see such a mess?"

Those were the first words uttered by Marie Calumet when she had taken possession of her small chamber at the top of the stairs, the scene of Curé Lefranc's memorable encounter with Suzon in her nightgown. The exclamation, flung in the face of the good Curé Flavel and his darling niece, could hardly be construed as a compliment.

It should be said here that to understand the value of this utterance from the mouth of Monsieur le curé's new housekeeper, the reader must realize that Marie Calumet's frankness was at times quite undistinguishable from rudeness. When a thought entered her head, she immediately gave it voice, and whether or not people took offence worried her not in the least.

She abhorred dirt of any kind and, without further ado, set to work with a vengeance. A mere hour after her arrival at the rectory she donned a goose-dirt-colored housedress, started to cook pea soup enriched with large slices of lard, put a stew of pig's feet — one of the priest's favorite dishes — on the stove, and set to wash, dust, pick up, polish, scrape, wipe, wax, rub, brush, and sweep everything in sight.

A week later, the rectory had undergone a complete metamorphosis.

There was not a speck of dust left on the furniture, the floors gleamed in golden hues of straw, windows sparkled in the sun. Stove, pots, and pans shone like mirrors; the dishes were neatly stacked in the large cupboard. And a mere glance at the bedrooms, now so tidy, so clean, so white, was enough to produce a yen for a nap.

Even Monsieur le curé, who was usually punctual as a sundial, was fifteen minutes late for Mass the first time he took his rest in the large spindle bed made up by Marie Calumet.

Once again, the flowers and plants lifted up their heads. The hens pecked with gusto, and the rooster remembered his long-forgotten ardor. The cat Fifine, on the other hand, deprived of her excesses in the now solidly padlocked milkshed, was no longer quite so rotund.

The priest felt ten years younger. He had recovered his appetite enough to tuck away four meals a day.

But do not blame him, dear reader. It was all the fault of this confounded servant, for she was a cook without peer. And, best of all, she could not only make rhubarb wine, but her brew was better than anyone else's.

Income now exceeded expenses. And this also was incontestably due to the talents of Marie Calumet. At last, Monsieur le curé found himself relieved of all his worries by this faithful and intelligent administrator of the rectory and its cares, and he raised his arms to heaven in daily jubilation, "Oh, my apparition! My apparition!" There was not one villager who was not acquainted with the cause of his happiness.

It was barely five o'clock. Not quite awake, the day had opened but one eye; soon the sun would cast its fiery rays upon nature. Along the sides of the road, the tears of the night clung like silver sequins to every blade of the short grass, and in the large, tufted trees, the good-for-nothing sparrow shook his sleep-benumbed wings. From the top of the dungheap by the stable, the purple-crowned rooster, king and herald of the courtyard, rose on his mud-caked claws and proclaimed the birth of a new day.

"Marie soak your bread
Marie soak your bread
Marie soak your bread
In the gravy.
Marie soak your bread
Marie soak your bread
Marie soak your bread
In the wine..."

It was Monsieur le curé's hired man, humming to himself as he came trotting down the road. He looked a little forlorn this fine morning.

Narcisse was a sturdy man. His back was slightly bent, his face and neck sunburned. He wore a red and black calico shirt in the Bavarian style and the cowhide boots commonly called Indian boots. He walked along with his head bent, sad as a dog who has just been given proof of his masters's affection with a kick in the rear.

Narcisse had entered into the service of Monsieur le curé Flavel at the age of eighteen and could be counted amongst the fixtures of the rectory. He had done his daily chores, without ambition and without ill will, for close to a quarter of a century and, in all that time, had earned only one honorable mention — one memorable morning, his master had compared him to the model servant in the Holy Bible. This manifestation of the curé's appreciation had brought a ray of sunshine into the monotony of his life.

"Eh, Narcisse! What's got into you this morning? You look like a man who's lost his loaf of bread!" Narcisse raised his head and recognized the schoolmaster leaning out of the window of his garret to test the temperature. Every morning, at the same hour, the same nightcap appeared in the same window frame of the little house.

"Ah, my dear M'sieu, say what you will, there's no one like her!"

"What are you babbling about?"

"Well, you know, Marie Calumet."

"Of course. That explains everything. And who, pray tell, is Marie Calumet?"

"Are you telling me that you don't know Marie Calumet, M'sieu? Why, the whole congregation knows her already! Now there is a woman for you! Ah, M'sieu, if only you could see her! She's got bearing... and class... and aplomb... and she can make you a pea soup, but a pea soup I tell you..."

To underscore his admiration, Narcisse ended his eulogy on a long, drawn-out whistle.

"My word, Narcisse! It looks to me as though you've gone and fallen in love!"

Like a man with a guilty conscience, our enthusiast blushed to the roots of his hair and beat a hurried retreat. "Cripes! Now that's a good one. Me? Falling in love at forty-three? You must be joking, my dear M'sieu. Me, fly in the face of everybody and start the whole parish gossiping?" Realizing that he was about to talk himself into a corner, Monsieur le curé's hired man abruptly broke off the conversation and went on his way. Anger was beginning to rise in him.

A little further on, he came upon the imposing Marcelline, who was on her way to the river bank with an enormous basket of dirty clothes.

"Hello, Narcisse! You sure look bedraggled this morning!"

The angry mood went from bad to worse. "Now that's a good one. I'll have you know, Ma Marcelline, that I've never felt happier."

"And where would you be shuffling to so sadly, Narcisse?" This time it was old man Lanoix, on the way to his barn.

"I'm going to the blacksmith to get a new handle for my axe."

"Why can't they leave me in peace?" the poor fellow muttered between his teeth. "They're more tiresome than a roomful of fortune tellers."

The blacksmith shop of Saint Ildefonse had been open for at least half an hour and work was in full swing. Roaring like a Cyclop, the furnace was vomiting flames of hell. A barefoot lad, whose pants were held up by shoulder braces, hung on the bellows. Every time he came down, he seemed to be sending up a gust of wind cutting through the chimney.

A pair of harnessed draught horses stood waiting to be shod. The blacksmith, a colossus of a man with hairy, muscular arms, his shirt open to his navel under a leather apron, came down on the anvil like a demon, oblivious to the flying sparks that grazed his skin. He had just given the final hammer blows to a horseshoe and, having dipped it in cold water, was nailing it to the hoof of a restless stallion, squeezing the animal's leg between his thighs.

Near the door a Newfoundland, muzzle resting on his paws, warmed his flanks in the morning sun.

"Morning, Narcisse," said the blacksmith, looking up from his work. "And what kind wind blows you here today?"

"I've come to bring you my axe handle to repair. Yesterday that old fart of a verger came to bend my ear with his vile talk. Well, I told the good-for-nothing muttonhead not to come babbling and slobbering with his silly stories or I'd let him have the worst drubbing he ever caught. And he answered, 'Don't you play the strong-armed guy with me, or you'll catch a slap in the face.' Well, I was splitting wood just then, and I swung the axe so hard that I went and broke it."

The blacksmith looked at Narcisse with unabashed astonishment. "You, Narcisse?" he asked, "You did that? Go on with you, old scab!"

"Well… I was just going to tell you, the handle was cracked already."

"But that's not what I mean. You — you never get mad! What did the verger say then, to make you lose your temper like that?"

Had Narcisse been prepared for this question, his lips would have been sealed. He began to fidget. "He said… he said to me…" he mumbled.

"Now, now," said the blacksmith, determined to worm the truth out of Narcisse. "What have we come to when Monsieur le curé's hired man goes around keeping secrets, and at this late date, too."

"Oh well… well… he said that Mamzelle Calumet, M'sieu le curé's housekeeper, was probably not half as good as everyone made her out to be."

"And what difference does it make to you, if the verger says things like that? You wouldn't perchance be in love with Marie Calumet?"

"Don't say stupid things like that, eh? Is it true then that you can't find anyone to your taste anymore without people saying that you've gone and fallen in love before you've had time to light a pipe? When are you going to give me back my axe anyway?"

"Come by later today if you like."

"And make it cheap."

"One shilling."

"That's not what I'd call cheap. But I don't care, it's Monsieur le curé who pays."

Narcisse stomped off, muttering curses at the whole world. He hadn't gone a hundred yards, when some joker who had been waiting at the blacksmith's called after him at the top of his voice, "Eh, Narcisse. Do I hear wedding bells?"

Chapter VI

Marie Calumet's Matador

When Narcisse, gesticulating like an irate madman, returned to the rectory, he suddenly found himself face to face with Marie Calumet.

"I beg your pardon, Mamzelle..." he murmured.

And there he stood, in great confusion, rolling his large straw hat between his earth-stained fingers, and feasted his eyes on the beloved woman. Oh, he loved her indeed, as she stood there before him holding two milk pails in one hand and one of those small milking stools in the other.

"Good morning, M'sieu Narcisse," she replied. "Nice weather we're having."

"Oh! Yes, Mamzelle."

"We'll get a lot of work done today."

"Oh! Yes, Mamzelle."

"Would you be nice, M'sieu Narcisse, and go call my cows? They've gone off into the neighbor's field. The gate was open and the greedy things just wandered over."

"Sure, I'll get them for you," Narcisse replied eagerly, feigning self-assurance.

Actually, courage had never been one of Narcisse's dominant traits, and he could sense that throwing himself into the pursuit of cows in such distinguished company was not at all a promising undertaking. Still, here was Marie Calumet, standing right beside him, and it would not do to hesitate.

He straightens himself up with pride and throws out his chest. Just as the matador enters the arena, smiling under the eyes of the beloved mistress, so Narcisse sets foot on the soil where he will give undeniable proof of his courage and devotion to the object of his ardor and his sighs.

He is, however, nervous.

From a distance — oh, a good distance — he waves his hat and calls, "Hey, cows! Hey, cows!"

Marie Calumet's dear creatures, swatting flies with their tails, merely turn a placid eye towards their interlocutor, then resume their grazing without giving further consideration to his invitation. Having failed in this first attempt, Narcisse ventures forth another thirty feet where success eludes him once more. The bull, on the other hand, has deigned to take a few steps in his direction, and that is not a very encouraging development for our matador. As his hesitation increases, the unfortunate Narcisse — he is now sweating profusely — wonders anxiously where this cow hunt will lead him and why did he not linger in bed another half-hour this morning.

For an instant — oh, only a single instant — he considers capitulation. But when he turns his head, he sees Marie Calumet still looking at him and beside her the verger who, on his way to ring the church bell for Mass, has stopped to witness this innocent spectacle, whose potential for melodrama has not escaped him.

"He must be shaking in his boots," Zéphirin cackles, hoping to ridicule the man destined to become his rival in Marie Calumet's eyes.

"Why don't you go and give him a hand, then?"

The prudent verger ignores this exhortation. "There isn't time. I'm late for Mass as it is. Otherwise I'd..."

He pretends he is leaving. Only, he stops after a couple of yards and leans over the fence. The spectacle is too good to miss.

A heartrending scream, a desperate cry rend the air. Narcisse, in a sublime thrust — oh love, how numerous are your victims — has come too close to the cows, and the bull, head down, has taken aim.

Now he forgets all, the coward: Marie Calumet, her bearing, her aplomb, her class, even her pea soup. His life is at stake and it must be saved.

He no longer runs, he flies. Here, at last, is the fence. Only one leap to salvation but — oh, misery — a large deep ditch, a devil of a ditch bars passage.

More dead than alive, he throws himself in another direction. He zigzags like a rabbit, falls, scrambles to his feet, stumbles, regains his balance. And all the time he can feel the fiery breath of the accursed bull on his neck. As happens in all moments of supreme peril, the details of his life parade in flashing visions before his haggard eyes...

Then he sees himself caught, gored, pierced, thrown into space, disemboweled, trampled, a bleeding, shapeless mass, brrrr... A veil seems to unfold before his eyes and everything wavers and blurs. The end has come. But no, on his right there is another fence and no ditch. Come on, Narcisse! One last effort.

Five Masses for Saint Joseph and a candle for the gracious Sainte Anne!

The fugitive scales the last obstacle and rolls to the bottom of a trench. He closes his eyes. He is soaked to the skin. No matter, he is safe at last!

In this pitiful state, the unfortunate Narcisse rises to

a vertical position once more. Close by, Marie Calumet is laughing so heartily that tears are streaming down her face. The verger is doubled over with mirth.

"You should be more careful, Narcisse," he shouts, running towards the church, "or you'll get yourself gored. Oh, you're a sight!"

Narcisse was entirely covered with a mixture of slime, muddy water, and dung. And yet, his fall, his mad run, the bull, the cows, even that pest of a verger — all were as nothing compared with the shame he felt when he had to face Marie Calumet. To be seen by her in this condition! Dear God, what humiliation!

And she for whom he had covered himself with dung and shame was laughing!

The farmers coming to Low Mass all stopped and surrounded him. Even the priest lingered for ten cruel minutes.

"Alas, poor lad," Marie Calumet managed to say at last, trying to look compassionate but unable to stop laughing. "Alas, poor lad, I do feel for you. That was quite a feat! Oh, you're bleeding!"

Narcisse had scratched his forehead on a stone.

"Quick! Quick! You must change your clothes and lie down, or you'll catch a bad fever!"

What could he do but obey her? Still, in all his misery, he showed a touching concern for her. "You won't be able to milk your cows," he said.

"Sure I will. Take a look."

The cows were there, not two feet away, mocking him with their large calm eyes. They had returned of their own will, because such was their pleasure.

"The wretches," he moaned, shaking his fist. And seeing the bull who was trotting back to his own pasture, "You! If I ever lay hands on you!"

Hounded by the guffaws and jokes of the farmers, he

sheepishly fled to the rectory and climbed to his small garret, where he undressed and went to bed.

Now that he was alone, the hired man fell to thinking, and it did not take him long to make a terrible discovery. It stunned him.

Narcisse loved Marie Calumet.

It had come over him like a whiplash, he would explain later. But Marie? Did she love him? And yet, he had thought...

The stairs creaked under a firm step. "Could it be her?" thought Narcisse.

It was. She carried a bowl of warm milk in her own two hands.

"It's funny, Mamzelle," he stammered, "but when I saw you, I felt my heart beat and flutter like a frightened bird."

"There you are," she said and handed him the dish of milk. This will make you feel better. It's straight from the cows, you know the ones..." And she burst out laughing again.

"I've earned it for sure," remarked Narcisse. "Those beggars! They certainly gave me the runaround."

He drank his milk, watching Marie Calumet out of the corner of his eye. She straightened his blanket and dressed the wound on his head with one of her own handkerchiefs.

"My heart feels quite swollen," he thought. "It'll burst for sure." He would have liked to take her hand in his and tell her that he loved her. But he was too shy and said nothing.

Letting his head fall back onto the pillow, he merely murmured, "Thank you very much, Mamzelle Marie."

Chapter VII

Wheat or Hay?

For at least a fortnight now, discord had reared its head among the peaceful parishioners of Saint Ildefonse and to avoid the more violent forms of combat, such as cudgel blows and pitchfork gorings, they engaged in a lively battle of the tongues. Some contended this, others rejoined that. Those who were crafty and articulate made speeches, those who could formulate no more than confused nonsense were tongue-tied and often remained silent.

That summer, most of the farmers had sown the greater parts of their lands with hay, and it had been a particularly abundant crop. But the grain crop was not showing much promise. Therefore, the reader will understand why the farmers, especially those who had sown only hay and thereby found themselves unaffected by the traditional tithe of grain, did all they could to promote this form of tithe over one that would be applied to hay.

They failed to understand why they should be forced, now any more than in years past, to pay their tithes in any form other than with every twenty-sixth bushel of grain.

On the other hand, the parish bigots and the churchwardens had appointed themselves champions of Monsieur le curé and came to the defense of his rights with the ferocity of bare-fanged Cerberuses.

Just because hay was now the principal crop, they argued, was no reason to use a cheap subterfuge, deprive their priest of his income, and make his position untenable.

Who would have believed that the driving force behind this argument, which had thrown the otherwise so peaceful village of Saint Ildefonse into the heat of controversy, was none other than Marie Calumet?

But then again, why not? Have there not been, since the beginning of time, predestined beings, whose task here on earth is to fulfill some grand and sublime mission? Is not woman the beginning and the end of all things?

Sainte Geneviève saved Paris, Joan of Arc, France. Why should not Marie Calumet save the curé and his rectory from the ruin which now threatened both?

Admittedly, it was already late in the day, but Marie Calumet knew how to make up for lost time. To further her ends, she had already brought about some momentous developments.

At the moment she was laboring hard to restore some equilibrium in Curé Flavel's accounts, an arduous and thankless task since the priest insisted on giving more than he received. Do not believe, dear reader, that Marie Calumet was uncharitable. No, indeed, and *honi soit qui mal y pense*.

But she placed Monsieur le curé above charity, and when it was a question of Marie Calumet's curé, well then, by golly, there was only one thing to do — put down one's head and barrel past all the decisions made by the minister plenipotentiary of the rectory and the entire parish of Saint Ildefonse into the bargain.

53

To reach her goal, Marie Calumet resolved to attack, first of all, the problem of the tithe. She proposed to abolish the method of applying the tax exclusively to grain and rather to apply it to both hay and grain. She calculated that this fiscal maneuver would bring in a surplus of no less than four hundred dollars annually.

So far, no one in the parish had thought of applying this kind of arithmetic to the problem, not even Monsieur le curé — and if anyone should have it was certainly he. From time immemorial, faithful subjects that they were, the trusty parishioners of Saint Ildefonse had, in good years and bad, contributed every twenty-sixth bushel of grain and had always gone home pleased and happy with his benediction.

One morning as she was serving Monsieur le curé his barley coffee, Marie Calumet decided to submit her project of reform. But the priest, ignoring the fact that the plan had been conceived solely to put a little order into his affairs, received it rather coolly, thereby dealing a severe blow to her expectations and hopes.

He was worried... later perhaps... he would think about it. He did not wish to offend his parishioners. Certainly, four hundred dollars was nothing to sneeze at... he would see.

It was following this setback that the housekeeper, who had the pastor's interests more at heart than he did himself, undertook her secret and wily campaign.

Not wanting to turn the entire parish against herself, she decided that Monsieur le curé's hired hand would be her front man.

Narcisse, meticulously following the secret orders of his lady general, first approached the churchwardens, the blacksmith, the schoolmaster, the notary — in short, all those who did not cultivate an inch of soil — and, most important, a half-dozen old maids whose bigotry was equaled only by the volubility of their natterings and their passion for gossip.

Everyone played his part so well that two days later, when the pastor was apprised of the shadowy plot and wanted to put a stop to it, the entire parish was already up in arms. What grieved the saintly man most of all was that every parishioner, Marie Calumet excepted, was firmly convinced that Monsieur le curé himself was the author of the cabal.

This was how matters stood on the following Sunday, when the pastor made a decision which risked severing forever the excellent relationship and shared interest which had always existed between him and his remarkable housekeeper.

That Sunday, just as they did every other Sunday of the year, most of the men lingered on the church steps while awaiting the third call to Mass, talking about harvests, horses, livestock, and discussing the burning topic of the day — the tithe.

The tithe!

They felt ill at ease in their Sunday clothes. And they did indeed look comical in their eight-dollar ready-made city suits, with their tight sleeves and pants which barely reached down to their heavy boots.

All, without exception, had accessorized this outfit with sky-blue, apple-green, or tender-pink ties and crowned it with felt bowler hats or beaver caps. And not one, even the poorest among them, had forgotten his plaster or wood pipe with its imitation amber tip, a luxury acquired after many great economies.

In the square across from the church stood some fifty barouches, wagons, calèches, buggies, and carts. Each of the unharnessed horses had before it a sheaf of hay. Some of the more restive animals were tied to the elm and ash trees.

On the stoop of the church, the verger had just belabored the long hemp cord, ringing out the third call to Mass.

Two minutes later, the farmers had entered the temple.

The church of Saint Ildefonse was decorated in white and gold — dirty chalk-white and tarnished copper-gold. There was no rood screen, merely a pedestal for the organ. An enormous cast-iron stove rose in the dead center of the nave, its gigantic ducts undulating throughout the building.

The choirboys, in tired surplices and cassocks stopping at mid-leg, had taken up their places a few minutes prior to the arrival of the celebrant.

The heat on that Sunday was enough to melt the tallow candles in their glass chandeliers. Imprisoned in their niches, the chubby-faced, painted plaster saints were suffocating.

The women cooled themselves with fans of colored paper. The men mopped their foreheads with the large dusty handkerchiefs they had just spread over their knees to protect their fine Sunday pants.

To the outrage of the faithful, Marie Calumet, who had been busy preparing her lunch, arrived only in time for the Gospel. But being the center of attention did not even cause her to raise one eyebrow.

With her military gait, she strode down the entire nave without lowering her eyes and sat down in the front pew, near the communion rail. It was the pew reserved for the rectory household.

Chapter VIII

Marie Calumet is Not Pleased

When he had finished reading the Gospel, the curé adjusted his maniple and moved down in front of the choir. Having recommended the special intentions for the week and called the banns, the saintly orator made a large Sign of the Cross, which the faithful imitated.

This is how he began his sermon.

"My dear brothers:

" *'Redde Caesari quae sunt Caesaris et quae sunt Dei Deo.* Render unto Caesar that which is Caesar's and unto God that which is God's.'

" 'Whatever you may say, whatever you may do, always act for the greater glory of God.'

"I am certain, my very dear brothers, that these are the sentiments which have animated you during your recent discussion of a question which touches closely on the worship of God, since it allows His priests to live and gives them the means of transmitting His divine will to you.

"It saddens me greatly, my dear brothers, to be forced to speak to you of such worldly things from this high pulpit'' — there was no pulpit — ''but there are circumstances when we priests are forced to mingle the word of God with the vulgar aspects of life. It is as with the ox and the ass in the Bible; the law allows you to pull them out of the well on the Sabbath. But am I saying, dear brothers, that the tithe is then such a vulgar thing? Are you really giving this pittance to a man, to your curé? No, it is to God Himself that you are giving alms. Think of that, my dear brothers, think of the honor that is bestowed upon you, think of the Lord who holds out His hand to you until that blessed day when He will pay you back a hundredfold for everything which you have given to Him. The writings of the Evangelists abound with this promise. 'Amen, amen, I say onto you that whatever you shall give in My name shall be returned a hundredfold in heaven.'

"This small portion of your property which you give to the minister of God will be returned to you a hundred to one and will bring the blessing of heaven upon your lands for next year's harvest.

"And yet, these alms must not give rise to internal discord in a parish where calm and peace have always reigned. It has come to my attention, my dear brothers, that there is dissension amongst you these days, because some of you wish to go on paying the tithe in grain, whereas others would prefer to pay it in hay. It is also true that those who wish to pay with grain are very small in number. And so, taking into consideration the minority of the latter and not wishing to offend the majority of my dear parishioners, I have reached my own conclusion on the matter, and I say to you, since this is what you wish — so be it. Pay in grain."

A stifled exclamation, loud enough to be heard by many, followed these words. Marie Calumet was exceedingly angry.

"Now that's just a lot of nonsense," she muttered.

Sweating profusely, she fanned herself with small, jerky motions.

58

Monsieur le curé, who seemed not to have heard, continued. "Those who wish to see me about the tithe may do so this afternoon between one and three o'clock. Kindly use the side door which leads directly to my office.

"While we are on the subject of charity, I would like to take this opportunity, my dear brothers, to exhort you to open your arms to the needy followers of Christ who travel these parts, asking you for a crust of bread, a bowl of pea soup, or a slice of lard. I have, on the whole, only praise to offer you; you have already proved yourselves to be most charitable. That is good, and God will reward you for it."

At that point during the sermon, three or four of the faithful who were standing near the door at the rear of the nave tried to steal away.

At this, the priest's voice rose in anger. "Hey! My friends over there, I am not speaking to the chickens, you know. Kindly remain with us to the end of Mass. Don't you think that the word of God is meant for you as well as the others?"

Then he continued, "I have, however, received complaints about certain individuals, important members of our community, who have refused their help to these unfortunates on the pretext that they might be marauders. These people are afraid of beggars who ask for charity in the light of day, and yet they allow their daughters to go out at dusk and take long walks at great distances from their homes.

"My dear brothers, it is not prudent to allow your daughters to be out like this after sunset, just as it is not prudent to allow them to dance. Dancing is a pastime inspired by the devil; it serves only to excite the senses and will lead to sin.

"Ah, my very dear brothers, I cannot warn you

enough against this scourge. Dancing is one of the traps of hell laid for you by the spirit of darkness who stalks you ceaselessly, like a roaring lion, *quarens quem devoret.*

"And while we are still on this subject, I must warn you, fathers and mothers, against the perils of long courtships, which are another source of sin. When a young man comes to your home to woo your daughter, he will be well behaved at first. Gradually, he will become bolder and, in the end, youth will drift towards regrettable abuses.

"When an admirer calls at your home and you perceive that he has not made up his mind to ask for your daughter's hand, send him on his way. Do not fear to lose out on a match, however advantageous it may seem. You may be sure that there will always be others and your daughter will only have gained esteem.

"The salvation of your children is more important than a good match. Always remember the words with which Saint Francis Xavier, the Apostle of India, took his leave from this world. 'For what shall it profit a man if he shall gain the whole world, and lose his own soul?'

"This brings me to the story of the wretch who came from the city to a parish in our county some years ago. Posing as a suitor, he gained entry into the home of a worthy family, only to dishonor their child after a few visits. Having ruined the life of the poor girl and exposed her to eternal flames, the coward abandoned her. Let this dreadful tale, fathers and mothers, and you too, young girls who are listening to me, serve you as a lesson for the future.

"Next week, my dear brothers, His Excellency the Bishop will pay a pastoral visit to our parish. Give generously, for this is how you can insure seeing His

Excellency frequently. The bishop does us great honor in coming to visit our parish and I am convinced that you will receive so august a personage with all the honors due to his station.

"As I have said before, my dear brothers, when I spoke of the tithe, charity is one of the great Christian virtues. But in view of the great heat today, I will elaborate on the subject no more.

"Today, the collection will be taken up for the benefit of His Excellency who has consented to honor us with his presence. Be generous, dear brothers, do not attach yourselves to your worldly goods; in return, you will earn the kingdom of heaven which belongs to the poor in spirit. I pray with all my heart that this blessing may be granted you.

"In the name of the Father and of the Son and of the Holy Ghost. Amen."

When the Mass had ended, the villagers who had not yet gone to fetch their carriages from the square formed two lines outside the church to watch the women walk past, greet friends with a slight tip of the hat or a mere nod, and feast their eyes on the young girls.

Between these two human hedges, Marie Calumet passed like a thundercloud, pushing people out of her way and looking at no one, not even the unfortunate Narcisse.

And to think that to please his beloved, the unhappy lover had bought a thirty-cent tie and a bag of sour drops only the day before!

The curé's hired man had left the church a few moments before the end of Mass. For the past five minutes he had seen nothing, heard nothing. His heart pounded so violently that his chest seemed to be bursting. He was lying in wait for Marie Calumet, hoping that she would allow him to accompany her to the rectory.

When she came out at last, he offered her his arm and mumbled, "Would you allow me, miss..."

"Get away from me!" barked the housekeeper and swept past him.

The verger, who had just rung the bell and was now standing on the church steps, witnessed the rebuff and burst out laughing. Worse, he was joined in his mirth by others who had seen the incident. For a moment, the furious and dejected Narcisse thought that he would strangle Zéphirin. Barely controlling himself, he muttered through his teeth, "I'm not the type to go around picking fights, but that blessed verger, I'm going to settle all my accounts with him at one clip any day now."

"Hey, Narcisse," whispered the blacksmith with a twinkle in his eye and an elbow in Narcisse's ribs, "how goes the romance?"

Narcisse merely raised his eyes to heaven and did not reply. There were two reasons for this. The first was that he did not appreciate the joke in the least; he was in no laughing mood at the moment. The second was that on Sundays and holy days Narcisse was not merely Narcisse but "Monsieur Narcisse." Everyone, including the curé, had to respect this rule. There was no reply for those who did not.

At first, Curé Flavel had been annoyed by this silly idea, as he called it. But even he had to capitulate before the mute obstinacy of his hired man.

And so, short as it was, Narcisse had to cross the distance between the church and the rectory all alone. With clenched fists and sorrow in his soul, he made for the barn, where he threw himself on a pile of straw and gave way to his anguish.

In front of the church, the women were chatting before returning to their carriages. They inquired how things were going — if this one had bought something, if that one had heard from her daughter-in-law, if the father who had been in a bad way and not long for this world was getting better at last. The young girls giggled and gloated over the handsome lads of the parish, uttered cries of surprise and envy upon hearing of an approaching wedding, and invited each other for an evening's fun when the hay was harvested. Here and there, a buggy or cart stopped in front of a frame or fieldstone house. Folks embraced, exchanged greetings and, on leaving, cried, "Come and see us! Drop in anytime!"

When Marie Calumet returned to the rectory, she immediately berated the curé's niece who, her prayerbook still under her arm, stood near the fence alone with Gustave, the blacksmith's son, a solid lad of handsome build and gentle eyes. This sight only served to exacerbate the housekeeper's irritation. She could not abide the young man.

"That loafer! That good-for-nothing," she would tell Suzon a hundred times a day, "should stick with his own worthless lot. That skirt-chaser is after every girl from one end of the parish to the other. There's no having truck with people like him and if I were M'sieu le curé, I wouldn't even let him come near the rectory."

Storming into the curé's house, Marie Calumet threw her hat on the dining-room table, flung her shawl (which seemed to emit a sob at this harsh treatment) on the floor, and plunked her gloves on a shelf between two potted mignonettes. Then she sat down and rose again, fell to pacing, sat down once more, fidgeted, grumbled, growled, stormed, stamped her foot in anger, and waited with feverish impatience for the priest, who was taking his time coming home.

Oh, she was angry!

Meanwhile, the soup was burning. The potatoes stuck to the bottom of the pot. The stew thickened like glue.

"It doesn't make sense!" she repeated over and over again. "He is digging his own grave! I can talk and talk and he won't listen to me at all!"

Puffing like a seal, the curé at last came up the front stairs of the rectory. Marie Calumet did not wait for him to enter. She ran up to meet him. He could already hear thunder and lifted his head as though a cloud were ready to burst and unleash a hailstorm upon him. His face fell.

"Well, M'sieu le curé, you've really done it this time. You can be proud of yourself."

"How do you mean, Marie?" asked the curé, looking worried.

"How could you do it, M'sieu le curé! You could have had a surplus of about eight hundred crowns this year if you hadn't gone and spoiled it all!"

"Come, come, Marie, don't let a little thing like this upset you."

She rose to her full height. "A little thing! Ah, M'sieu le curé," she groaned, wiping her eyes, "here I work myself ragged to put a little order in your life and you keep pulling us down every time!"

"Now look, Marie," the pastor retorted gently, "you know very well that I could not do otherwise. There would have been talk in the parish. It would have been said that I let myself be guided by material interests."

"Well if that was your reason, M'sieu le curé, you made a big mistake. D'you believe for a minute that they would see it that way? You know very well that they couldn't care less. Why couldn't you handle this like your neighbor, M'sieu le curé of Saint Apollinaire? Now there's a man with a little business sense! Did he back down when his parishioners came to him and asked to pay their tithe in grain? They won't forget in a hurry what he did, and that's for sure. And more than that, d'you know what else M'sieu le curé Lefranc does?"

Marie Calumet lowered her voice and came closer to Curé Flavel. "You may not believe this, M'sieu le curé, but he makes loans at fifteen percent. And what's more, instead of selling the grain his people pay him in the fall at the going price, he stores it until spring so that those who are short of grain have to borrow from him at the price of twenty-five pecks for twenty pecks. I can assure you, M'sieu le curé, that he collected a jolly good tithe the following autumn. I heard this from my cousin Jerome 'cause he's one of the ones that got caught.

"And I tell you this with all respect. M'sieu le curé, but if you didn't suit me like you do, well then, by golly, I swear to God, I'd pack my bundle and that would be the end of it. There!"

Curé Flavel had a sincere affection for this good woman who was so completely devoted to his interests. And so, unlike most pastors, who cannot suffer the slightest contradiction nor the merest reprimand, he replied with a smile. "All right, all right, Marie, I'll try to do better next time. In the meantime, go check the potatoes. They smell horribly burned."

"Well, all right then, M'sieu le curé," apologized the housekeeper, starting for the kitchen. "I'm sorry if you have to eat burned potatoes. But it's your own fault, M'sieu le curé, it's your own fault!"

Chapter IX

A Sacrifice to End All Sacrifices

We come now to a memorable date. It would take the imagination of a Chateaubriand, the wit of a Daudet, the graphic vision of a Loti, the verve of a Richepin to recount this day, a day destined to become a milestone in the life of our heroine.

We learn from the lives of great men and women that, in the twilight of their years, they select from memory this day or that and call it the most beautiful of all. Marie Calumet, on her deathbed, would clearly remember the three most beautiful days of her life: her arrival at the rectory, her first meeting with the bishop of the diocese and... but let us not anticipate.

After so many years, Marie Calumet was now about to experience a long dreamed-of happiness, a happiness which would fulfill the yearnings of her soul and quench the thirst of her heart. She would see His Excellency at close range at last, she would touch his cassock, perhaps she would even speak to him. Let death and terror follow, what would it matter to her? She would expire with peace and serenity in her heart since she would have heard from her bishop's lips words addressed only to herself.

Monsieur le curé Flavel had announced the visit of

His Excellency the Bishop this week at Saint Il-defonse. Now, in the eyes of our rural populace, an episcopal visit to the country is an event of supreme importance. It is among the great religious festivals in the ecclesiastical calendar of the village and woe to anyone so imprudent as to dare to downgrade its importance. No victorious emperor returning to Rome on his triumphal chariot drawn by snow-white horses, no Frankish king in golden armor entering the good city of Paris on his charger to bear news of victorious battles, no miracle worker setting foot on a hospitable beach, heralded by tales of supernatural deeds, was acclaimed with the exaltation with which the folk in our part of the country welcome their bishop on a pastoral visit.

When the memorable day dawned, Marie Calumet was the first to thrust her head out of the window. She wanted to make sure that the weather would be beautiful. Unfortunately, it seemed to her that an unfriendly breeze blew from the southeast and that the grayish sky did not augur well.

Alarmed, she joined her hands and, raising her eyes towards heaven, prayed with fervor. "Oh, sweet Jesus," she implored, "you can see that the weather is mucking up, can't you? Please, accord me the grace of clearing it up, and I promise you I will make two Stations of the Cross!"

Half an hour later, the sun found an opening in the dawn mist and set the entire horizon ablaze.

If the housekeeper did not believe in miracles, she nevertheless found herself privileged by the Lord, since the elements seemed to obey her slightest wishes.

By five o'clock that morning housework was already in full swing, though on the eve of the holy visit Marie had given the rectory such a thorough cleaning that even the most inquisitive search would have failed to discover a single particle of dust.

Yet once more, this morning, she dusted every piece of furniture and swept out every corner.

Imagine! If His Excellency were to be dissatisfied! If he were to find cause to criticize the condition of the rectory! What torture!

If, on the other hand, he were to compliment Monsieur le curé on the cleanliness of his home! Oh, then her humble country girl's soul would glorify the Lord for centuries and centuries to come!

Seven o'clock. The rectory is humming with activity. The comings and goings do not cease. Curé, verger, hired man, and housekeeper meet only in passing, call out to each other, run, speak only when necessary. Nevertheless Narcisse invents a thousand excuses to find himself in Marie Calumet's path.

The villagers come and go, their faces bathed in sweat, some armed with hammers, some with saws, some with axes. They enter the home of their priest without knocking, without taking off their hats. For a brief moment, they have set aside the customary religious awe with which they present themselves at the door of the rectory. Today they could pass for a band of seditionists in full revolt against the Church, revolutionaries who are making ready to tear down the rectory, having first slain its tenant.

But they are only our good friends from Saint Ildefonse. They are it is true, a little heated, a little excited by the imminent arrival of His Excellency, but what they have come for is to take orders from their pastor or, more precisely, from his housekeeper.

In the midst of all this activity, Monsieur le curé's niece slept on with grim determination. Angered and shocked by such indifference, Marie Calumet climbed the narrow stairs, grumbling to herself.

Broom in hand and without knocking, she entered the girl's room. "Come now, Mamzelle Suzon, how can you still be in bed with His Excellency expected here shortly. After all, you're not suffering from consumption. We've been at work downstairs and outside for hours already!"

The curé's niece stretched and yawned before she answered in a thick voice. "Never mind the bishop. I've got plenty of time."

"Heavens! How dare you speak like that of His Excellency? Come, come, this is no time to play the lady. Up you get! Start moving and hurry about it a little. Get down there and help me with my work."

And suiting action to word, Marie Calumet, with a brusque and cruel motion, pulled the blankets from the bed and opened the tightly shut blinds.

A breath of fresh air, redolent of newly cut hay, filled the room.

Far from reacting as expected to this brutal awakening, the pastor's niece merely pulled her nightgown, which had immodestly risen during the night, down over her feet. Only when she could think of nothing better, she rose, taking care not to hurry too much.

Monsieur le curé's second-in-command had already left. She had stepped out on the porch for a moment to catch a breath of fresh air and observe the villagers who were putting the finishing touches to the outdoor decorations.

"Start over with this!" she ordered. "Take down that pavilion over there! Plant this pine elsewhere! Hang this garland a little higher! What are you trying to do? Get His Excellency caught on his tassels?"

They all obeyed without a murmur.

Both sides of the road were lined with tall markers. These markers were young shoots of birch or maple simply planted, foliage and all, on icy rivers or snow-covered fields and, as a rule, served to indicate either a danger to avoid or a path to follow. During the summer season, however, their character changed from the utilitarian to the aesthetic. On such holidays as an episcopal visit, the Feast of Corpus Christi, or our national holiday, Saint Jean Baptiste Day, they served to brighten the roads of a village with a double row of green foliage.

The more affluent members of the parish, whose homes featured soaring flagpoles, had raised the tricolor and the flags were fluttering in the morning breeze.

The old village doctor had even gone so far as to prepare a surprise for his priest. He had hoisted the Vatican standard and a flag bearing the bishop's escutcheon. This delicate gesture from a loving son of the Church would no doubt give great pleasure to His Excellency. There was no better way to dispose him favorably towards one of his subjects.

Crisscrossing the road from eave to eave, blood-red and vivid blue streamers glittered in the sun, bearing gold-lettered inscriptions, such as "Long Live His Excellency," "Blessed Be He Who Comes in the Name of The Lord," "Hosanna," "Gloria in Excelsis Deo," "Let Us Praise Our Bishop," and "Glory to the Envoy of God."

It goes without saying that, in Saint Ildefonse, no one worked on that great day.

All the villagers were decked out in their Sunday finery and looked exceedingly festive indeed.

Even the carriages had undergone a thorough scrubbing — immersed in the river up to their axles — and now sparkled in the sun as they came rolling up the long, gray road. The horses were curried and brushed,

70

their ears adorned with brilliant red paper rosettes. Spurred on by whips decorated with handsome new streamers, they trotted down the road with their heads held high.

Overnight, the road had been transformed into a race course; and the villagers, who were passionate horse lovers, challenged each other with steadily mounting bets.

Many vehicles groaned under the weight of several generations: grandfather, grandmother, father, mother, sons, daughters, grandchildren. At every jolt in the road, the axles threatened to collapse under this human mass.

Holding his reins with an air of nonchalance, the blacksmith's son caught almost every eye in the crowd. For who should be sitting beside him, looking as fresh as an armful of lilacs, but the pastor's blond niece? Proudly, he cracked his whip and had a wink for everyone.

"Just watch me," he thought, "for there's no doubt that the most beautiful girl in the village is sitting beside me."

Meanwhile, Marie Calumet was shaken by an inner conflict.

Pleasure and duty were locked in mortal struggle.

As was the custom in all good houses, Narcisse had been delegated by Monsieur le curé to meet the bishop and to greet him in the name of his master, the proprietor of this rustic manor, otherwise known by the humble name of rectory.

The hired man had asked his idol to join him in the execution of this pleasant duty.

To meet her bishop in this manner would have been for Marie Calumet one of those joys, one of those happy occasions that come only once in a lifetime. She would have burst with pleasure had she been able, dressed in her best finery, to be a member of the sacred delegation. The sacred delegation of Monsieur le curé!

Her imagination took flight. She could even hear the hurrahs of the masses, hurrahs that would not all be for His Excellency. Some of the acclamation might even be meant for her!

And why not?

Was she not a bona fide member of the rectory?

On the other hand, the voice of duty, albeit shaky, was calling, supplicating, imperious, irresistible.

For Marie Calumet, the price of honor had to be paid in self-abnegation.

It was her duty to stay at her post, to supervise the final details in the rectory, and to see to the preparation of a feast worthy of the majesty of the august personage who had consented to visit his flock.

It was a sacrifice to end all sacrifices, but the good Lord would no doubt take note.

Unfortunately Narcisse, whose intelligence was limited and whose own soul could not conceive of such pinnacles of self-denial, misread the refusal of his Dulcinea. He concluded that Marie Calumet was rejecting even his slightest efforts to hold out the hand of platonic friendship.

Ah! Had she but known what fermented in this skull, had she but understood the agony of this wounded heart!

Chapter X

What to Do With
His Excellency's Holy Piss?

The procession advanced with majesty. Following a
rustic cavalcade, the bishop's coach, drawn by two
horses whose tails and manes had been braided with
narrow red and blue ribbons, now hove into view. At
the sides of the road, the crowd was kept at bay by a
troop of ungainly horsemen.

The prelate, a shriveled man with a sweet smile
sketched on his glabrous face, was comfortably en-
sconced on a garnet-colored velvet cushion. Through
the lenses of his gold-rimmed spectacles he cast a
pleased glance upon the jubilant crowd.

Occasionally, in response to the crowd's acclama-
tions, he deigned to raise his episcopal hat, whose
splendid tassels the folk alongside the road were pointing out to each other with admiration.

Here and there a good woman would fall to her
knees, an old man would touch his brow to the dust.

At this, the bishop's hand, adorned with an egg-
sized amethyst, would trace a large Sign of the Cross
under the pure blue sky.

Monsieur le curé of Saint Apollinaire, honored by
His Excellency's request, was seated next to his pre-

late. Facing them sat the mayors of that village and of Saint Ildefonse.

They would speak of this day to their children's children! One of the sons of the mayor of Saint Ildefonse, who had won first prize in free-hand drawing at the village school, would later immortalize the unforgettable scene on paper.

Behind the coach of honor, in order of merit and distinction, followed the dignitaries of the parish, followed, in turn, by a host of villagers, all crowded into sixty-odd vehicles.

Now, the episcopal cortège entered the cobbled street between the two rows of houses which constituted the village proper. Joining in the village's infectious joy, the churchbells rang out lustily from the tower of the humble temple.

The coach turned towards the church. As His Excellency made ready to step down, two hundred of his faithful lambs rushed towards him. He barely missed being carried in their arms to the throne which had been built in front of the church.

The episcopal throne of Saint Ildefonse merits special description. It was made from one of those ancient, high-backed commode chairs.

The honor and duty of decorating the bishop's throne had fallen to Marie Calumet. She had covered its orifice with a pillow of red cotton, which she had enlivened with small gold paper stars.

"There," she had reassured the priest, "His Excellency is going to be in seventh heaven."

But when His Excellency rose to grant his blessing to the faithful prostrated at his feet, one of these small asteroids remained fixed to a region of his anatomy where stars are not customarily placed as an emblem of inspiration and genius.

74

Luckily for ecclesiastical dignity, this incident passed nearly unnoticed.

The *Te Deum*, bellowed by a dozen-odd choristers, was followed by the collection, which, in sincere praise of the villagers of Saint Ildefonse, we must admit was very generous. Accompanied by his retinue the bishop now betook himself to the rectory.

Lured by the hopes of a copious meal — one that promised to be without precedent, if one was to believe Marie Calumet's reputation as a cordon bleu cook — several pastors from neighboring villages had meanwhile appeared on the scene.

Needless to say, Marie Calumet was not about to disappoint the expectation of this elite. She had prepared a feast of which the annals of the rectory keep a fond and awestruck memory to this very day.

Even the bishop, of whom it certainly cannot be said that he nourished himself with crusts and root beer, sent his compliments to the housekeeper who, second to His Excellency, of course, had suddenly become the heroine of the day.

Marie Calumet lost her head completely. In her confusion she turned as red as a beet. From the bottom of her heart she vowed boundless gratitude to the bishop of the diocese. Her fondest wishes had come true at last. Not only had His Excellency spoken to her, but he had said, giving her a friendly tap on the cheek, "My daughter, you are the best cook I have ever come across. Monsieur le curé has sung your praises, and I can only say that they are entirely deserved."

The other priests, anxious to follow His Excellency's example, followed suit and lavished compliments on Marie Calumet.

I will pass in silence over certain civilities in the course of which the table companions set out to prove that man, regardless of what social hierarchy he belongs to, is only human after all, and that a good meal is one of the pleasures of humanity.

His Excellency, as was the custom, planned to administer the Sacrament of Confirmation to the children of the parish the next day. This necessitated an overnight stay at the rectory for the saintly man. And, of course, the rectory of Saint Ildefonse could in no way double as a fashionable country inn.

Faced with this emergency, Monsieur le curé had not hesitated a second. He held council with Marie Calumet, for he could no longer manage without his housekeeper and never undertook the slightest action without first having sought her advice.

She knew the answer to everything.

Thus it was decided to make room for the visitor. Monsieur le curé would relinquish his room next to the parlor on the ground floor, to the bishop; Marie Calumet would give up her chamber to the priest; and the niece, the pretty Suzon, would absorb the entire shock of the migration and share her small iron bedstead with Marie Calumet.

Naturally Suzon, who liked her comfort, looked at this arrangement with a jaundiced eye.

Yet, what choice did she have but to submit to the all-powerful triple will of the bishop, the curé, and Marie Calumet?

The housekeeper was overcome with happy anticipation at the thought that tomorrow she would sleep in the very same bed in which Monsieur le curé would take his rest tonight. How many, among a hundred thousand, can claim to have enjoyed the same privilege, the same favor? Here, for her, was a means of coming closer to what was sacred...

And when the pious woman was making the beds the

next day, her emotions simply played havoc with her.

In all justice to her it must be said here that her feelings and the anticipation of all these promised pleasures were entirely virginal and platonic.

It is difficult to describe the profound emotion which seized her when she entered the episcopal chamber and, tremulously, set to cleaning it.

With religious awe, she took up the chamber pot as though it were a prize jug and prepared to empty its golden-brown contents into the common vessel through which pass all liquids of this kind. Suddenly she froze, perplexed...

"Bishop's piss!" she thought. "Now that must be something sacred."

What was she to do with it?

She sat down on the bed, placing the container on the floor in front of her. Staring at it fixedly, she began to think.

For a long time she sat motionless, reflecting on the problem. Certainly she could not dispose of it as one would of mere water.

It would be sacrilege...

On the other hand, could she leave it in the room? That would be neither clean nor hygienic...

For a moment, Marie Calumet thought of bottling the precious liquid. But did she have the right?

Unable to reach a conclusion, she took up the chamber pot once more, with infinite care, and went to seek the advice of the priest, who was cutting tobacco in his study.

"M'sieu le curé," she said mysteriously, holding the vessel out to him, "what shall we do with His Excellency's holy piss?"

Curé Flavel stared at his servant in amazement, wondering whether she had taken leave of her senses.

Then he burst out laughing.

But just as he was about to inform her that the precious liquid was to endure the common lot, he heard the voice of the bishop, who was coming towards the study.

The situation was dramatic indeed. There was not a moment to lose. Like the valiant soldier who seizes the half-burned fuse of a grenade and throws it to safety, so the gallant pastor grasped the chamber pot and flung it out the window.

It was at this precise moment that Monsieur le curé's hired man was passing below. Fate decreed that both the receptacle and its contents should land on his head.

The unfortunate Narcisse raised his eyes. All was quiet above.

"Why me?" he asked, and a tear ran out of the corner of his eye. "Why me? I didn't do anything!"

Chapter XI

In Which Narcisse Brings Influence into Play

A complete transformation had taken place in the manner and temperament of Narcisse; he was no longer the same man.

From the happy-go-lucky fellow he had always been before Marie Calumet's arrival at the rectory, and especially before he felt himself scorned by the one he loved, he had become taciturn and misanthropic. He no longer ate. He no longer slept. He was wasting away.

As can be expected, this abrupt change in the hired man's personality gave fresh fuel to the ever-alert gossip mills of the village.

The blacksmith, Suzon, and the verger, more perspicacious in these matters than the priest himself, wasted no time in discovering the cause of this deterioration in Narcisse's formerly happy disposition.

Naturally it did not take long for the entire village to become party to the open secret that Monsieur le curé's hired man was eating his heart out with love for Marie Calumet, and that the flame he carried inside him was slowly but irremediably destroying him.

What was so remarkable about this whole affair was that the pastor's housekeeper, to whom Narcisse, of course, had never dared avow his passion, was the one

person who remained unaware of this grievous afflic-
tion. Perhaps her numerous reforms inside and outside
the rectory had not left her enough time to notice this
detail, which certainly cannot be said to have been
lacking in importance.

If only she had known the immensity of the love
Narcisse bore her, if only she had known that this love
was slowly destroying the poor lad!

One fine morning, after a night of tossing and turning in his sweat-drenched bed, longing for a little love
and a little sleep, the ill-fated lover reached a decision.

Starting from the premise that a man reaches his goal
more easily with a little influence and protection than
he would without them, he contrived to find himself
alone in the presence of the curé, just as the latter was
returning from Low Mass. He would plead for Monsieur le curé's support in resolving the problem which
threatened to ruin his life.

Near the small side door of the vestry, he approached the priest, hat in hand. "M'sieu le curé...
M'sieu le curé..." he said, "I've come... I've
come..." Overcome with timidity and shame, he
stared at the tips of his moccasins and dared not continue.

"Of course, you've come," answered the curé.
"That's clear as the day to me. But why?"

"M'sieu le curé, I'll tell you. To make a long story
short, I've come to see you on my own private business."

"Well, if it's your own private business, it's none of
mine, is it?" The pastor prepared to continue on his
way towards the rectory.

"Well, darn it, M'sieu le curé, I've come... I've
come... because I need your help."

"Why?"

"If you please, M'sieu le curé, it'll take just a minute. I'll tell you… it's because I'm in love."

"Is that so? Better late than never, I always say. Is it true then what everyone is saying, Narcisse? That you've got your eye on my hired girl?"

"Yes. What can you do, M'sieu le curé?" Like a culprit who confesses his crime, Narcisse blushed and hung his head.

"Have you spoken to her, then?"

"M'sieu le curé, I haven't got the courage. I would like you to speak to her first."

Monsieur le curé, who was, after all, accustomed only to being the intermediary between God and man, felt ill at ease in the role of mediator in this amorous intrigue.

"And what do you want me to tell your lady love?"

"Speak well of me to her."

Curé Flavel promised somewhat evasively that he would do his best. Narcisse thanked him effusively and returned to the rectory.

In the kitchen he found Suzon who, for once, had risen early. She was playing with the cat, tickling the animal's belly.

Resolutely he went towards her.

Come what might, he would not leave one stone unturned in his quest for success.

"Mamzelle Suzon," he started, "what do you think of marriage?"

For a number of reasons, this question startled the young girl. The first was that Narcisse had never before opened his mouth on this burning subject.

She answered with ill-concealed longing in her eyes, "I think it must be a jolly good thing."

"Because, y'know, Mamzelle Suzon, I would like to get married."

"You? Get married?"

"What do you mean? Can't I get married like everyone else?"

"Sure you can!" Suzon admitted, laughing. "But who'd you want to get married to? There... oh, of course, how silly of me! I'll bet it's Marie Calumet!"

"Exactly. Who else would it be if not Marie Calumet?"

"And what does your Marie Calumet have to say?"

"What can she have to say? She has nothing to say because I haven't asked her."

"You haven't asked her? You want to marry Marie Calumet and you haven't told her that you love her?"

"Well, I'll tell you, Mamzelle Suzon, I haven't the courage, y'know."

"But you have to tell her, big dummy!"

"I know, I know. But you know, I'm afraid that if I tell her, I'll say dumb things."

"You have to tell her, and the sooner the better. Ah! Would I ever like to be a man!" exulted the young girl. "I'd do so many things that I can't do now. Would I ever like to be a man! Would I ever like to be a man! It must be nice to be a man, eh, Narcisse?"

Narcisse's mouth dropped open. He was at a loss for words. Still, Monsieur le curé's hired man did not wish to pass for a simpleton.

He ventured a nonchalant approach. "Frankly, Mamzelle Suzon, as far as I am concerned, it doesn't make any difference whether you wear pants or petticoats."

"Petticoats are nothing but a nuisance. You get all tangled up in them."

But Suzon promised support, and Narcisse went on his way happy and confident.

Suzon was possessed of an unhealthy curiosity, and

her indiscretions, in which naivety mingled with an itch for the unknown, had already brought the wrath of her uncle and pastor down on her head.

With each reprimand she promised to reform. Alas, her words were but idle talk, and soon she would begin to misbehave again.

On one occasion, Monsieur le curé's holy wrath had been so much aroused that she had come close to being banished from the home where she had spent so many happy years. That day, the pastor had been summoned to attend to some poor devil who had received a mortal kick from a vicious horse. He had been reading the Holy Scriptures at the time.

He had left in great haste, barely taking the time to put on his hat.

Once before, he had surprised his niece leafing through the Bible and he had torn the good book from her hands violently. On the evening in question, the young girl had been on her way to her chamber and, looking into the study, had seen her uncle steeped in reading the book which, according to him, was so dangerous for her.

He had left the book open at the Canticle of Canticles. Suzon, who had not yet gone to bed, had heard her uncle leave.

Since she was not tired, she had left her bedroom and paused for a moment at the top of the stairs.

She had tiptoed downstairs, hearing only the monotonous tic-toc of the large inlaid clock in the corner of the curé's study.

What had made her act this way? Nothing, if not the healthy curiosity inherent in human nature. She had moved towards her uncle's desk and there had seen the imposing tome whose reading was forbidden to the majority of the faithful. The actual possession of this forbidden fruit had filled her with an indefinable emotion.

She had approached the book, much as an ephebus would approach a woman about to give herself to him for the first time, and sat down. Skipping some of the verses, her eyes had devoured the most captivating:

Let him kiss me with the kiss of his mouth: for thy breasts are better than wine....

Behold thou art fair, O my love, behold thou art fair, thy eyes are as those of doves.

Behold, thou art fair, my beloved, and comely....

As the apple tree among the trees of the woods, so is my beloved among the sons. I sat down under his shadow, whom I desired: and his fruit was sweet to my palate.

He brought me into the cellar of wine, he set in order charity in me.

Stay me up with flowers, compass me about with apples: because I languish with love.

His left hand is under my head, and his right hand shall embrace me.

I adjure you, O ye daughters of Jerusalem, by the roes, and the harts of the fields, that you stir not up, nor make the beloved to awake, till she please....

I will rise, and will go about the city: in the streets and in the broad ways I will seek him whom my soul loveth; I sought him, and I found him not....

When I had a little passed by them, I found him whom my soul loveth: I held him: and I will not let him go, till I bring him into my mother's house, and into the chamber of her that bore me....

Thou hast wounded my heart, my sister, my spouse, thou hast wounded my heart with one of thy eyes, and with one hair of thy neck.

How beautiful are thy breasts, my sister, my spouse! Thy breasts are more beautiful than wine, and the sweet smell of thy ointments above all aromatical spices.

Thy lips, my spouse, are as a dropping honeycomb, honey and milk are under thy tongue; and the smell of thy garments, as the smell of frankincense.

My sister, my spouse is a garden enclosed, a garden enclosed, a fountain sealed up....

Arise, O north wind, and come O south wind, blow through my garden and let the aromatical spices thereof flow. Let my beloved come into his garden, and eat the fruit of his apple trees.

I am come into my garden, O my sister, my spouse, I have gathered my myrrh, with my aromatical spices: I have eaten the honeycomb with my honey, I have drunk my wine with my milk: eat, O friends, and drink, and be inebriated, my dearly beloved.

I sleep, and my heart watcheth: the voice of my beloved knocking: Open to me, my sister, my love, my dove, my undefiled: for my head is full of dew, and my locks of the drops of the nights....

I opened the bolt of my door to my beloved: but he had turned aside and was gone. My soul melted when he spoke: I sought him, and found him not...

I adjure you, O daughters of Jerusalem, if you find my beloved, that you tell him that I languish with love.

What manner of one is thy beloved of the beloved, O thou most beautiful among women? What manner of one is thy beloved of the beloved, that thou hast so adjured us?

My beloved is white and ruddy, chosen out of thousands....

His hands are turned and as of gold, full of hyacinths....

His legs as pillars of marble that are set upon bases of gold. His form as of Libanus, excellent as the cedars.

His throat most sweet, and he is all lovely: such is my beloved, and he is my friend, O ye daughters of Jerusalem....

I to my beloved, and my beloved to me, who among the lilies....

One is my dove, my perfect one is but one, she is the only one of her mother, the chosen of her that bore her. The daughters saw her and declared her most blessed: the queens and concubines, and they praised her.

Who is she that cometh forth as the morning, fair as the moon, bright as the sun, terrible as an army set in array?...

How beautiful art thou, and how comely, my dearest, in deligths!...

I to my beloved, and his turning is towards me....

Put me as a seal upon thy heart, as a seal upon thy arm, for love is strong as death, jealousy as hard as hell, the lamps thereof are fire and flames.

Many waters cannot quench charity, neither can the floods drown it: if a man should give all the substance of his house for love, he shall despise it as nothing....

I am a wall: and my breasts are as a tower since I am become in his presence as one finding peace.

Devouring these pages with a shudder, Suzon had become so engrossed that she had neither seen nor heard the curé return home.

She had just read the last verse.

"Suzon!" her uncle had thundered, in a towering rage.

"The young girl, who was wearing her nightgown, had been violently startled.

86

The priest had been furious. "These are things that you don't need to know. I forbid you, I repeat, to put your nose into any of my books."

Holding back the tears which were appearing at the end of her long blond lashes, the poor child had taken flight as swiftly as the deer — or rather the doe — on the mountain of spices.

Meanwhile, Monsieur le curé, in the interest of prudence and thinking with good reason that to withold forbidden fruit from a woman is to invite her to taste it, had placed all the books he considered off limits under lock and key in his bookcase.

Chapter XII

A Homeric Struggle
Between Two Amorous Rivals

On the very next day, when he saw that Suzon had not yet spoken to Marie Calumet on his behalf, Narcisse reiterated his request.

"I beg of you, Mamzelle Suzon, put in a little word for me with Mamzelle Marie."

"Shall I tell her that you want to marry her?"

"No, no. Not quite yet. But you can tell her that I love her a whole lot."

"Why don't you come with me, then? You won't have to say anything. I'll do all the talking for you."

"Oh, no! I tell you, Mamzelle Suzon, I'd be too embarrassed. You talk to her first. That way we'll see what she has to say."

"Suzon! Suzon!" the housekeeper was heard calling at the top of her voice. "Suzon! Suzon!"

Suzon, absorbed in the confidences of the hired man did not or did not seem to hear.

Mohammed, as the reader well knows, once ordered a mountain to come to him; the mountain, of course, did not move an inch. Faced with this fact, the Muslim prophet could do no better than go to the mountain.

When Marie Calumet realized that her calls had fallen on deaf ears, she decided to go to the young girl.

She appeared in the doorway of the kitchen surrounded by a flood of sunlight. Her sleeves were pushed back to her armpits, her stout arms dripped soapy water, and her washday-red hands held a pair of cotton underpants which belonged to none other than Monsieur le curé's hired man.

Startled by this unforeseen development, Narcisse made a hasty exit through the dining-room door.

It was washday at the rectory, and Marie Calumet was doing the work of ten.

In the outbuilding next to the dairy, near the gigantic bread oven, lay a mountainous heap of dirty clothes — the priest's thick, gray wool socks; the hired man's undershirts; Marie Calumet's camisoles and petticoats; Suzon's pantaloons; huge bedsheets in the coarse weave of the country; pillow cases; and handkerchiefs, large as flags, in a myriad of colors and checks.

Steam rose slowly from the washtub, a movable wooden receptacle, resting on a trestle on which it had to be pushed back and forth by the housekeeper and the curé's niece.

Like the team of horses in the fable, both were sweating and panting, both were nearing exhaustion. Water trickled down their faces, which were strained with heat and fatigue. Clouds of suds, to which the sun had lent a polychrome hue, flooded the rustic laundry and splashed onto their cotton dresses, outlining their bodies as though they were undressed.

The young girl's hair had come undone in a moist braid and circled her neck, attractively framing her face in which mischievous eyes sparkled like two lumps of coal.

Now the movement of her snow-white arms began to falter; she was no longer pushing the arm of the washing machine with her former strength.

At last, having reached the end of her breath and strength, Suzon collapsed onto a flour sack.

She stretched out, tired and lazy. "I'm exhausted!" she moaned.

A few feet from the young girl, the verger, returning from the vestry, was passing by. Through the large side door, she called out to him, "Hey, Zéphirin! Come here and take my place for a few minutes. It won't kill you for just this once!"

Zéphirin was a slothful creature, a shortcoming for which he was frequently criticized.

"Come on!" said the young girl, rising from her flour sack. "You'll have gotten over it by the time you get married."

To entice the lazybones into replacing Suzon for ten long minutes, the reward would have to be irresistible. And love, we believe, was such an enticement.

Oh yes, dear reader. Love had indeed entered the verger's heart like a gnawing worm.

A strange charm must have emanated from the complex personality of this Marie Calumet. She had only been at the rectory two months, and already there were two rivals for her love. And what rivals, dear Lord!

Truth to tell, Zéphirin was not a handsome man. He was cross-eyed and pockmarked as a sieve into the bargain. But Zéphirin was only thirty years old and already held a distinguished position, for he was a member of the religious elite of Saint Ildefonse.

He even had a refusal of marriage to his credit. For nearly seven years now, the daughter of the village butcher had been eating her heart out for him. And one evening, without much ado, just like that, she had even asked him to marry her.

Zéphirin's refusal had been categoric.

Let us confess here that the misunderstood damsel

had passed her thirty-fifth birthday and that she possessed a hunchback that would have been the envy of the
bellringer of Notre Dame.

And now, Monsieur le curé's verger was about to
spend ten minutes in a tête-à-tête with the housekeeper. Suzon, moreover, obliged by leaving the shed,
for she had just seen the blacksmith's son signaling her
from the side of the road a short distance from the
rectory.

At first, Zéphirin seemed to have swallowed his
tongue; he let the housekeeper be, without opening his
mouth. Finally, embarrassed by his very silence, he
cleared his throat. "Mamzelle Marie, hum... Mamzelle Marie, hum... Mamz... did you know that you
are a fine figure of a woman?"

"Quit joking, will you!"

"Upon my word! But when I tell you this, Mamzelle
Marie, I wouldn't dream of joking. And furthermore,
listen to this, you only have to see the look in the eyes
of the fellows around here to get what I mean. And,"
he added, pushing the arm of the washing machine more
vigorously, "I don't think I have to tell you any more."

"I wouldn't know about that," Marie Calumet answered naively," but I think that the fellows here must
act pretty much the same way they do where I come
from."

"I've no right to give you advice," said the hypo-
critical verger, "it's none of my business, but I would
caution you to be on your guard. There's some pretty
bold people around here."

"Go on with you! You know very well that I'm past
forty and that girls of my age don't believe that kind of
talk."

"Oh, is that what you think? Well, let me tell
you..."

He had stopped working and taken a few steps towards the housekeeper. He was now speaking directly to the underside of her chin. Marie Calumet, to use an old Canadian saying, could have eaten her bread off the top of his head.

Narcisse, oh irony of fate, passed the shed at this very moment. He was on his way to harness the rectory horse.

He saw Zéphirin standing close to Marie Calumet and perceived in his rival's crossed eyes the flame of desire and passion.

For the first time in his life, Monsieur le curé's hired man felt indescribable hatred and jealousy rising in his heart.

To see Zéphirin so close to the one for whom, day after day, he was eating his heart out, made him seethe with anger.

Of course, this man was the obstacle!

Were they perhaps making plans together? Perhaps even laughing at him?

Was it perhaps their doing that, a few days ago, the chamber pot had fallen on his head?

"There's a limit to everything," he muttered, grinding his teeth. "And the time to get even once and for all is now or never."

The moment was favorable. Worried by Zéphirin's excitement, Marie Calumet had dropped the conversation and had left the shed in search of the curé's niece, muttering that the child was worse than a cat and could never be counted on to stay in one place.

"Hey! You, over there," Narcisse called out to Zéphirin, "you sure like ogling the women, don't you? Always under the skirts of Mamzelle Marie!"

"Go chase yourself, you old dumbbell! I can ogle

any woman I like and there's no need for you to stick your nose into it!''

"I can stick my nose anywhere I like and there's not a thing you can do about it!''

"Is that what you think, eh? One more word out of you and I'll..." Zéphirin showed his fist to the fuming Narcisse.

"Don't be stupid!'' muttered Narcisse.

"Ah, you piss!'' replied the verger scornfully.

"Is that so? Well now, you had better come behind the barn and I'll show you a French Canadian with fur on his paws!''

Narcisse's bravery, as I have already mentioned, was not unlimited. But on that day he could have mustered the strength and courage to knock down an enraged bull with his bare fists.

"Ah!'' he yelled as he headed for the barn, followed by Zéphirin. "You think you can call me a piss, eh? We'll see about that. Because I'm going to knock your block off!''

In order to keep the fires of their belligerent passion going, the two adversaries heaped abuse on each other until they reached the battlefield.

Our two gladiators were now within the confines of the arena. When I say arena, I am referring to a corner of the vegetable garden bounded by the two parallel structures of the barn and the stable. The audience were not now a bloodthirsty emperor, effete and dissolute courtiers, haughty and debauched patrician ladies, bathed in milk and perfumed with spikenard, and the stamping, screaming populace. *Minora canamus*.

No, Narcisse's and Zéphirin's spectators consisted of a few hens and a cock astray in the tomato patch, of carrots and parsnips, a couple of turkeys, and three or four pigs wallowing in the sty two steps from the stable.

Suckling conscientiously, a piglet, on hearing the approaching noise, let go of the maternal teat. Then, having satisfied himself that none of the hostile manifestations was directed at him, he returned to the task with half-closed eyes and a grunt of pleasure and contentment.

The two pugilists removed their hats and coats, rolled up their sleeves, and threw themselves upon each other without further ado.

The battle was brief.

Narcisse forcefully applied his fist to the nose of his rival and sent him rolling into the grass and stinkweed. Zéphirin rose, his face smeared with blood.

Reaching out for each other, they went into a clinch. Their breaths mingled, veins stood out on their reddened necks, their shirts were torn to shreds.

Narcisse freed himself at last and was about to administer a fearful blow to Zéphirin when the latter, with his free hand, grasped his enemy in a region south of the belt, a maneuver which is, of course, forbidden in the Marquis of Queensbury's Rules.

Crazed with all the despair of rage and pain, Narcisse now directed a left hook onto the eye of the coward, instantly causing him to see stars and to go down for a second time.

The hired man did not give him a chance to rise again.

He straddled Zéphirin's chest and held down his arms.

"Is that enough for you, you swine?" he yelled.

"Yes," groaned the other, feebly.

Meanwhile, the two copper hands of the great rectory clock had passed the number twelve, and yet no bells were announcing the Angelus.

Awaiting the echo of that cherished sound to take a short break and have a bite to eat, the farmers mused that noon was certainly taking its time today.

Monsieur le curé, who never sat down to lunch without being summoned by this bell, was pacing the dining room impatiently, wondering what the delay might be.

He looked outside.

"I would like to know what has happened to my verger," he thought.

Suzon was hungry. She was also furious with the verger whom she disrespectfully referred to as an "old pumpkin."

Marie Calumet, too, thought that something was amiss. It was, after all, the first time in the history of Saint Ildefonse that the Angelus had not been heard. She decided to go out and look for the man who, at this moment, was on every villager's mind.

When she reached the stable, she uttered a cry of shocked surprise and stretched out a gentle hand in a pacifying gesture.

"Oh, gracious Sainte Anne! How can people hurt each other like that! I beg of you, Monsieur Narcisse, show a little Christian charity!"

At the sound of this enchanting voice, Narcisse rose quickly, pushing self-denial to the point of holding out his hand to his adversary.

How mysterious is the power of love that it can soften the harshest resentments, the most violent hatreds!

Zéphirin refused the hand of his foe.

"I wonder why she came here," thought Narcisse on his way to the rectory. "Was it for me, or was it for Zéphirin?"

Chapter XIII

A Somber Day
in the Life of Marie Calumet

The outcome of the fist fight between Marie Calumet's rivals had not been at all what Narcisse had expected.

The priest's hired man, who had never so much as lifted a finger to anyone, had fully expected to be severely trounced in the contest.

Instead, he had given his adversary a lesson the latter would remember for a long time to come.

Blood had flowed, and Narcisse was satisfied that his honor had been preserved.

But the verger would live forever with the memory of the humiliating position in which he had been found by Marie Calumet.

Reconciliation, from that day on, was out of the question. One might as well have asked the two lovers to renounce their desire, and neither was prepared to take such drastic measures.

Thus, two of Monsieur le curé's subjects, though members of a holy household, would henceforth ignore each other's existence completely.

On the other hand, the incident had plunged the naive soul of Marie Calumet into a state of great confusion.

The curé's servant had a philosophic turn of mind

which was most surprising for a person of her ilk. She liked to discover the reasons behind every event.

Narcisse and Zéphirin had had a set-to, of that there was not the shadow of a doubt. She had seen blood flow from the verger's nostrils, seen the squinting, half-closed eye and the bewildered look it had given to his face.

But why had they fought?

That is what Marie Calumet wanted to know. Because, after all, people do not slug each other for nothing, and if these men had done it so pitilessly, their reasons for doing so must have been serious.

Once the housekeeper had reached this conclusion, she held on to it as tenaciously as a starving dog holds on to a bone.

But it was all too much, even for her. The onrush of sudden emotions had left its mark upon her constitution, and when the constitution has been shaken, revolution sometimes follows.

So it was with Marie Calumet.

Our heroine found herself obliged to enter one of those small, wooden shacks built in our countryside to allow mankind to pay nature the tribute which is her due.

At the rectory of Saint Ildefonse, such a small shack was located next to the piggery; its users could not enter the one without passing through the other. It was, therefore, imperative that they close the door of the pigsty behind them.

The boar, sow, and piglets, like all living things, gloried in the thought of freedom and liked nothing better than to venture beyond the confines of their captivity.

Installed on a throne more rustic than that of Our Orator of the Fields, Marie Calumet watched a large green fly zigzagging through the fetid air. It was buzzing morosely.

It was during this moment of solitude that she had a strange premonition.

The big fly drummed the message into her ear. She had forgotten to close the door of the piggery. The entire dynasty had flown the coop.

"Gracious Sainte Anne!" she exclaimed in terror, "I forgot to close the door of the pigsty!"

And she rushed out in great confusion.

The door was indeed wide open, and Marie's premonition, alas, only too true!

The pigs, four in number — father, mother, son and daughter — had just escaped the cesspool called their retreat and were wandering hither and thither in the grass of the rectory's large courtyard.

So far, the family had been strolling together as a group, but when they saw the enemy, in the person of the housekeeper, giving chase, they panicked and disbanded.

A stampede ensued.

For five long minutes, Marie Calument galloped in pursuit of the rebels. The pigs, now uncontrollable in their quest for emancipation, took the direction of the King's Highway. There was no telling where their adventurous escape would lead.

The housekeeper now lost both her patience and her head. There was a stick within her reach. In a trice, she had bent down and picked it up. The first fugitive she caught up with was one of the piglets.

She administered an energetic thrashing to the piglet's back. Terrified by this unexpected ambush, the poor little creature, with its pink muzzle and curly tail, buckled, uttering pitiful cries.

The mother had already reached the highway. On

hearing her son's lamentations she shuddered to the core of her maternal entrails. Resolutely, she returned and faced the housekeeper with a threatening grunt.

The menacing stance did not intimidate Marie Calumet in the least. It was the sight of the whimpering piglet, sadly dragging its hind legs, that nearly broke her heart.

She crouched down and took the animal's head in her hands, which were weak and trembling with excitement, and laid her red cheek, on which two tears of sorrow and remorse rolled down slowly, against the muzzle of the young pig.

"Don't bawl, little one," she wept. "I didn't do it on purpose, and... and you know... don't worry... we'll all take good care of you."

Squealing mightily, the piglet turned a deaf ear to these consoling words, coming though they did from the kindest heart in the world.

In an outburst of tenderness, the housekeeper now gathered the piglet into her arms and, pressing it against her breast, carried it all the way to the pigsty.

From the stable, she fetched some fresh straw, which she spread out in a shady corner, and deposited the wounded hero on this downy bed. Finally, with a deep sigh and a look full of pity, she returned to the rectory.

But let us return to our other pigs.

On hearing Marie Calumet's desperate calls and the grunts of the mother pig, Narcisse and Zéphirin momentarily forgot their grudge and came running to the aid of the woman in whose name they had just done battle.

They succeeded in returning the recalcitrant animals to their former domicile.

Marie Calumet, meanwhile, had been completely

unhinged by the drama in which she had participated, indeed, had played the leading role.

In vain did she try to banish the somber vision from her mind. The sight of the little pig dragging its feet again and again intruded mercilessly upon her tormented soul. Again and again, its pitiful whimpering rang out in her ears.

Even the silence and serenity of the large rectory kitchen did nothing to lift the weight of Marie Calumet's intense sorrow. Looking out the window, she saw Monsieur le curé's hired man, hat in hand, the expression on his face betraying the burden in his heart.

"Mamzelle Marie..."

"Narcisse..."

"Mamzelle Marie..."

"What?"

"Mamzelle Marie..."

"Oh woe is me!" exclaimed Marie Calumet, and her eyes and mouth opened wide. "You've come to see me about the piglet."

"The piglet? The little piglet..."

"Yes! The little piglet that ran away and whose back I've broken."

"Ah, yes, he's in a very bad way... he's very low, the little piglet, Mamzelle Marie..." Like a friend who must tell a wife that her man just had his spine crushed in a fall from a crane and tries to break the news as gently as he can, so Narcisse chose his words carefully.

"I'll never believe it!" Marie Calumet sighed.

"So low, Mamzelle Marie, so low that I don't believe he can pull through."

"Oh Jesus, Mary, and Joseph! Is it possible? Can it be possible?"

Narcisse saw that the time had come to confess the whole truth. "Mamzelle Marie… I have to tell you. He is… the little piglet is dead."

"Dead!"

Her throat constricted as though in a vise, and Marie Calumet collapsed onto the rag-stuffed chair, which was covered in a very old, flowered cotton print.

Narcisse was shaken to the core of his being. He ran to the kitchen for a pail of water and a rag and busied himself applying cool compresses to the temples of his beloved.

"Blood on my hands!" sobbed Marie Calumet, her eyes wild and haggard, "Blood!"

She tried to remove the accursed stains from her hands.

"He's dead! He's dead!"

"Ah, yes, Mamzelle Marie, he's dead. But, golly, you mustn't carry on like this! After all, it was only a piglet."

It is easier to explain the housekeeper's despair if I point out that she had developed a spontaneous affection for the handsome little animal with its yellow, black-dotted skin and a muzzle as pink as a candy cane.

She had witnessed its birth. And it was she, who would not hurt a fly, who had slain it.

Its death, moreover, represented a serious loss to the rectory. A murdered pig, after all, is not the same as a slaughtered pig.

Well, she would have to economize on her snuff. For Marie Calumet was a snuff-taker, one of those snuff-lovers who never cease to fill their snuffboxes.

Chapter XIV

"Say What You Will, But I'll Never Believe That Girls of My Age Get Married!"

Dabbing the temples of the one he treasured in his heart, Narcisse gradually felt himself enveloped by a sense of well-being.

He would have liked to prolong the pleasant task indefinitely, had Marie Calumet not pushed him aside mildly and murmured, "My little pig! Thanks, that will do."

Narcisse's psychological insights were not of the broadest, but intuition told him that man must surprise woman in her times of emotional turmoil, because it is precisely then that she allows herself to show feelings she would otherwise conceal carefully.

A woman who is mistress of herself would never dare say or do what she will say or do in the heat of passion.

There was once a virgin, appetizing as a peach, who struggled in the arms of a man who had designs on her virtue. For just one weak moment, she ceased to labor in the defense of her honor. "What a nice ring you have there," she remarked on noticing a splendid diamond ring worn by her assailant. And she returned to battle, apparently determined to sell her skin dearly.

We must accept women as they are and not as they seem...

Monsieur le curé's hired man deemed the occasion opportune and resolved to make his grand move. He coughed, scratched himself, spat, coughed again, scratched again, spat again, and began.

"Mam... Mam... Mamzelle Marie..."

"What is it?"

"I think I have something to say."

"Then say it quickly, 'cause my potatoes are burning."

"Mamzelle Marie, I... I..."

Narcisse was unable to utter another word. With his head bowed, the pail half-filled with water in one hand, and the cloth with which he had been ministering to his friend in the other, he only looked foolish.

He was drenched in perspiration.

Marie Calumet grew tired of the silence and rose to add water to her kettle at the bottom of which the potatoes were burning.

Narcisse followed, but she turned away every time he came near.

He had to speak to her today, that much he knew; if he failed to act today, the opportunity would be lost forever.

"How beautiful she is!" he thought. Pouring boiling water into her kettle of potatoes she was indeed irresistible with her opulent figure, fresh skin, and red cheeks, on which two pearls of pity had gleamed earlier when she had learned of the little pig's death.

He set his bucket on the floor.

"Mamzelle Marie?" he ventured, taking one of her hands.

The housekeeper did not take her hand away; she lowered her eyes modestly.

It was a step forward, but the distance from the glass to the lips is great!

The curé's pretty niece slipped quietly through the dining-room door, surprising Narcisse just as he was about to confess his love.

How had her protegé found the courage to speak, she mused, when she herself had not yet opened her mouth on the burning topic?

At this moment Narcisse, who had happened to turn his head, saw Suzon. She motioned to him to take courage, not to become rattled. Turning the other way, Narcisse saw Monsieur le curé on the threshold of the kitchen door.

He felt intimidated by so many witnesses and was about to retreat when Curé Flavel, with mute gestures, gave him to understand that he should accomplish what he had set out to do.

Fortunately, he did not see the verger spying outside the window. Had he glimpsed those sneering, hate-filled eyes fixed on him, he would have capitulated immediately.

Our suitor finally took the awesome plunge.

"Mamzelle Marie," he began, "I've been wanting to tell you this for a long time, but there you are dammit… Oh, forgive me, forgive me, I meant to say 'holy cow.' No, that's not what I meant to say… For a long time now… well, there it is, Mamzelle Marie, I've been in love with you for a long time now, and I've never had the gumption to tell you."

There followed an unexpected and terrible incident. Marie Calumet had always been ferociously virtuous; the slightest aspersion on her modesty was enough to worry her, nay unsettle her completely.

At her age, Monsieur le curé's housekeeper could not conceive of a man's declaring his love for her with other than dubious intentions. If a suitor came to tell her "I love you," just like that, it must be that he was out for monkey business.

It was therefore her duty, as a good girl, to avenge the insult made to her virtue forthwith.

For one moment, only one brief moment, a flickering of pity touched her heart. But she overcame this momentary weakness and, raising a plump arm which was bared to the elbow, she administered the avenging slap on the cheek of the bold offender. It echoed through the kitchen of the saintly abode.

Narcisse was stunned. He was about to swear to the purity of his motives when the curé, his niece and the verger burst into the kitchen all at once.

"How could you, Mamzelle?" scolded Suzon, interposing herself between the housekeeper and the hired man.

As for the verger, he would not have traded that slap for two whole barrels of the sacramental wine, of which he secretly and regularly took an illicit sip.

"Good work, Mamzelle," he cackled. "Don't let just anyone bother you. He got what was coming to him. You were right to..."

Narcisse jumped.

"Shut your trap!" he roared. "You haven't forgotten the licking you just got, have you? Shut up if you know what's good for you!"

"He's right. You be quiet," added Suzon.

"Silence!" Monsieur le curé's voice dominated the babble like the thunderclap which precedes the approaching storm. "My home is neither a sugaring-off shed nor a hut for savages."

"You, first of all," he said, turning towards the verger. "You will be kind enough to go and ring Angelus."

"I'm going, M'sieu le curé, I'm going," replied the

verger serenely, with a malicious and triumphant look in the direction of his unfortunate rival.

Marie Calumet burst into tears.

The curé, Suzon, and the hired man all earnestly explained that if Narcisse had said that he loved her, it was because he wished first to court and later to marry her. But the idea of marriage was simply beyond Marie Calumet's grasp.

Go on with you! Who would even dream of marrying a girl her age, already past forty? And even if there existed a woman capable of inspiring passion at this advanced age, it was certainly not her!

She did not know her own power. She did not know that two men were tearing out their hair for her beautiful eyes, for her favors. That blood had been spilled for her and her alone, just as for the chatelaine of old heroic times.

Because Marie Calumet did not know her own powers, she failed to understand their impact upon her two knights.

In the end, she walked away from them all, muttering crossly, "Say what you will, but I'll never believe that girls of my age get married."

And as the bell started to ring out the Angelus, she put the soup on the table.

Chapter XV

Monsieur le Curé Gets
His Feet Wet in Lachine

One fine afternoon, Curé Flavel had gone to look up an old friend with whom he had lost touch for many years, but whom he had now discovered to be living in Lachine, a few miles from Montreal.

The two priests sat rocking on the front porch of the rectory, talking of the happy days of yore, which were, alas, quite far behind them. This conversation inspired the curé of Lachine, who adored poetry and poets, to recite these lines of Lamartine's:

"Oh why remember times gone by?
The winds will moan, the waves will leap.
But my sad thoughts, return to me;
I want to dream, but not to weep."

He was interrupted when two men, whose skin had been tanned by sun and wind, approached the rectory. They explained briefly that they were workers on a tow of logs, that they had come down from Kingston, that a mile upriver, on the tow they could all see over there, one of their comrades was dying and asking for Confession, and that they were on their way to fetch the doctor as well, so that they might all four go back in the rowboat to the dying man.

"Very well, my friends," the curé of Lachine replied quietly. "I shall meet you at the landing."

The two men saluted and rushed towards the doctor's house, whose door was surmounted by a gigantic mortar and pestle made of gilded wood that could be seen from a great distance.

The pastor of Lachine, whom Curé Flavel had agreed to accompany, was just putting on his hat and preparing to go down to the landing, when the two friends saw an old woman coming towards them. Her face was hidden in a handkerchief of red cotton with white dots, and her narrow shoulders were shaken by uninterrupted sobs.

Her boy, her only son, she said, was turning twenty-eight this fall. He had been helping out a neighbor who was putting a new roof on his stable. In order to nail down the shingles he had tried to sit astride the roof, had lost his balance, and had fallen to the ground.

He had fractured both his legs and his spinal column. And now he was twisting and moaning in agony, calling for a priest so that he might make his Confession before meeting his God.

Oh, the misery! Was it not enough that her man had been killed in similar circumstances not a year ago?

With the best intentions in the world and an indisputable apostolic zeal, the devoted priest could not be in two places at the same time. And yet, both cases seemed to be of extreme urgency.

When his friend lamented the unfortunate coincidence, Curé Flavel said calmly, "Do not torment yourself for so little, my friend. Follow this poor woman and I will bring the succor of our religion to the dying man on the tow."

Ten minutes later, he boarded the rowboat, along with the doctor and the two raftsmen, and they set off towards the tow which was now passing directly in front of the rectory.

Pulling the rowboat up behind them, they boarded the raft. At the sight of Monsieur le curé, every member of the crew removed his hat respectfully. Curé Flavel asked to be taken to the dying man immediately.

Slowly, the tow of logs floated downriver. Perhaps one of the most typical of Canadian scenes is a log train — or, to use the language of the trade, a tow — journeying down the Saint Lawrence and its rapids.

The convoy had left Kingston on Wednesday evening and had already negotiated the Prescott Rapids and those of Du Coteau without mishap or the loss of a single log. It had not yet, however, braved the Lachine Rapids, which were the most treacherous.

There was not a breath of wind. Not a trace of cloud was penciled against the deep blue sky, and the sun beat down like burning lead. The *Parthia*, a sturdy boat, was towing the logs at the end of a long cable.

Six long canoes, each carrying twenty Caughnawaga Indians, suddenly appeared alongside the log train.

These children of the woods rhythmically plunged their vividly painted oars, glistening in the sun, into the deep blue waves.

They approached with earsplitting chants and cries.

Pulling their canoes up behind them, the oarsmen boarded the raft.

A log train measures approximately three hundred and sixty by sixty-four feet, but it is broken up into five or six smaller rafts, called "pockets." They are made of balks or young saplings, layered and intertwined to a thickness of about four feet, held together by strong branches of wild cherry trees.

On each raft rises a mast, about ten feet high, onto which a sail can be hoisted when a breeze rises. Occasionally, this mast serves a very useful purpose — during the downward journey on the rapids, when the rafts are submerged, it provides support for the men to cling to.

A wooden cabin, divided into two parts, stands on the pilot's, or main, raft. This cabin serves many purposes — dining room, kitchen, bedroom, and, in stormy weather, shelter. Though not large, it can easily accommodate the entire team of men employed to bring the tow of wood from Kingston down to Montreal.

Actually, the only segments of the trip requiring many hands are those leading over the rapids. The remainder can easily be accomplished with seven or eight workers. To bring a tow of logs consisting of five rafts through the rapids, on the other hand, requires the work of no less than twenty-five or thirty robust men on each raft.

The bulk of the lumber comes from Georgian Bay. In Quebec City it is loaded aboard vessels bound for England.

Would the reader like to learn the cost of the transport of such a tow of wood, not including food for the men? The company pays twelve hundred dollars for the entire voyage — five hundred to cover the descent of the Lachine Rapids, four hundred for those of Du Coteau, and two hundred for those of Prescott. For this outlay, the company chalks up a net profit of no less than five thousand dollars on each shipment.

A wind had come up. The convoy was approaching the rapids, and the men set to the task of separating the rafts.

Twenty minutes later, the tow had been broken up into five rafts. Twenty-four oarsmen, twelve at the front and twelve at the rear of each raft, rowed with all their might in order to put enough distance between them so that they would not crush each other.

The pilot now raised his arms and the *Parthia* went full steam ahead to await the rafts at the foot of the rapids.

We are now very close to Heron Island. Already visible in the distance are the rushing waters, churned into snowy foam by eddies and pounding waves.

Now the rafts are sucked into a giant abyss where death itself seems to beckon to them with skeletal arms.

And here, in the midst of deafening noise, are the rapids.

It is the roar of the wild beast in the solitary night. Danger looms all around.

In every direction, the currents cross. Here is a reef just under the water's surface; there, a deep pool; further on, whirling with indomitable power, eddies in which death lurks. The men, thrown forward by one wave, are hurled back by the next.

It is the narrows between Scylla and Charybdis that they must cross.

The rafts are nearly submerged. Standing in water up to their knees, keeping well toward the front or back of the rafts, the oarsmen are bent over their large oars, which threaten to give way. Surely, they will smash themselves on those rocks, founder in those churning waters!

It is a *danse macabre* the rafts perform as they come down the rapids.

Another few moments and these brave men will have, once again, negotiated the abyss where so many unfortunate victims have left their bones.

"You'd better hold on tight, M'sieu le curé. We're all going straight to the devil!" shouted one of the oarsmen to Curé Flavel, who was leaning against the cabin.

"Have no fear, my good man!"

But a scream of horror suddenly rose from every throat. "Man overboard! Man overboard!"

The same oarsman who had warned Curé Flavel had, in turning his head, lost control of his oar. It had struck him in the chest, plunging him into the treacherous, howling waves of the rapids.

There now followed an unforgettable scene. Before anyone could guess at his heroic intentions, Monsieur le curé had torn off, rather than unbuttoned, his cassock.

He flung himself into the waves crying, "My Lord, have mercy upon my soul!"

Twice, the terrified crew saw him surface before he reappeared, the drowning oarsman in his steely grip. Both were carried off towards the foot of the rapids with dizzying speed.

How could they escape being smashed on the rocks, engulfed by a whirlpool? God alone knows.

At the foot of the rapids, the two men were pulled safely aboard.

"Monsieur le curé!" thundered the pilot, his voice breaking as he nearly crushed the priest's hands between his own, "come quickly, and have a little something strong to warm you. I tell you and I'm not lying, I would give ten years of my life to have done what you have just done, M'sieu le curé!"

"Fine, fine," answered the curé of Saint Ildefonse modestly. "Let's not talk about it anymore."

"Come, Nicholas," added the pilot to the oarsman

whom the priest had just rescued. "Come and drink a little drop to M'sieu le curé's health. And the rest of you, d'you hear, damn it all, there's enough for everyone today. Things like this happen only once in a lifetime."

Three cheers for Monsieur le curé!

"Hurrah! Hurrah! Hurrah!"

The five rafts had now passed over the rapids and were reassembled into a log train. The *Parthia* maneuvered in front to get them in tow.

Having acclaimed Monsieur le curé once more, the Indians boarded their canoes to return to Caughnawaga.

When the tow of logs reached Montreal, the curé shook hands with one and all and went ashore in company with the doctor and an oarsman.

There was a good breeze blowing now, and the small sails were hoisted. The tow of logs was on its way to Quebec City where it would arrive by Monday noon.

That same day, after supper, Monsieur le curé set out for his own village. No one was ever to learn of the humble pastor's heroic deed.

When Marie Calumet noted that his clothes were damp, he merely replied, "Oh yes, I forgot to tell you. I got my feet wet in Lachine."

Chapter XVI

Monsieur le Curé's Zouave

Barely two months had passed since Marie Calumet's arrival at the rectory of Saint Ildefonse. In that short time she had undergone more emotional upheavals than she had known in the course of her entire monotonous life in Sainte Geneviève.

A person of Marie's sort attaches considerable importance to everything which deviates from the ordinary course of events.

Imagine then, dear reader! Her arrival at the rectory, Monsieur le curé's sermon, the bullfight, the episcopal visit, the bishop's praises, the death of the little pig, Narcisse's declaration of love. In short, half of all this would have been more than enough to unsettle Marie Calumet in the most thorough fashion.

Ah, could she but lift the veil of the future and glimpse some of the joy, tenderness, and perils this mysterious destiny of hers concealed!

For several years now, our heroine had become pensive every time she laid eyes on a photograph. On every such occasion she would sit motionless, a finger held to her cheek and a gleam of longing in her eyes, and gloat over the zinc or cardboard reproduction.

She was like the tattered, barefoot little urchin who, on Christmas Eve, his nose glued to the bakery window, dreams of devouring the gingerbread santas and animals of colored sugar; she was even reminiscent of those other children, women, who are driven to ecstasy by stones sparkling like a thousand fires on the dark velvet of jewelry stores.

For the last two days in particular, Marie Calumet had been living in the clouds. The other members of the household were beginning to be most intrigued by her strange behavior.

As far as they could gather, the curé's servant must be suffering from the effects of recent events. How could they have suspected that, in fact, the cause of her preoccupation was a new-fangled invention called photography?

It was only too true.

Her spells of absent-mindedness were truly surprising.

"Marie," the curé would say, "bring me some coffee!" Marie would diligently fetch the mustard.

"Sugar, Marie." Marie passed the salt.

Were we to record the list of blunders the poor girl committed during that week, this book would never end.

One morning, when Monsieur le curé had asked for honey — he adored honey — Marie Calumet, with imperturbable aplomb, descended into the basement, searched for ten long minutes, and returned with a bottle of rhubarb wine.

On another day, she awoke late. Still prey to her ever-present obsession, she dressed in a twinkling and came down to the dining room where Monsieur le curé was already taking his breakfast.

"Merciful heavens!" he cried.

In a state of profound shock, he thrust his face into his handkerchief.

It would be impossible to describe the amazement of this chaste man. What was this terrible sight that had just shaken him to his roots? We must confess that there was ample reason for the priest to cover his face.

Crowning all her previous blunders, the housekeeper had forgotten to put on her skirt and petticoat!

She was appearing before her clergyman in the uniform of a pontifical Zouave, a nicely put-together Zouave at that, a veritable little drum major. It is easy to imagine the scene; there is no need to enter into details.

Having nibbled on the apple, our forebear, Eve, discovered that she was naked.

That was a pity indeed, for her daughters might have lived in sweet ignorance. Marie Calumet, it is true, was not completely naked, but we are forced to admit that her attire could hardly be called proper within these respectable walls.

So great were her shock and her shame that at first, she was unable to move. Gradually, her entire body began to tremble; her teeth chattered, and, arms flailing, she tottered upstairs.

It would have rent the reader's heart to see the despair of the unfortunate maiden. Her tears flowed freely; it was as though lascivious audacity and indiscretion had laid waste the sanctuary of her virginity with one stroke.

It would have been easier for her if she had been able to blame someone else for her misfortune; a woman who has voluntarily thrown modesty to the winds can shift the blame to another. But not Marie Calumet. She alone was responsible for her act and could blame no one but herself.

Only her boundless devotion to Monsieur le curé could have kept Marie Calumet in the rectory after this unfortunate incident. But for that devotion she would have slunk away, never to return again.

Suzon somehow had wormed the story out of her uncle and lost no time in passing the "secret" on to the blacksmith's son.

He, in turn, repeated it to Zéphirin who took malicious pleasure in communicating it to Narcisse. Two hours later, the entire village was freely discussing the story in every gruesome detail — Marie Calumet had, in the full light of day, given a lesson in astronomy to Monsieur le curé.

Gnawed by remorse and obsessed by the stern words of the Bible, "Woe be to him to whom scandal comes," quoted by the priest in one of his sermons, our virgin came to a desperate decision.

To mortify this lowly carcass of mud, which had but served to plunge her soul into eternal flames to the end of its days, she would enter a convent.

Not wanting to act too lightly, she went to see her confessor, secretly hoping that he would countermand her decision which, when she thought seriously about it, had about the same effect as an icy shower down her back.

Her confessor was, of course, none other than Curé Flavel.

But she could tell her confessor all kinds of things that she would never, never have dared mention to her Monsieur le curé, no, never!

The confessor, or rather Curé Flavel, did not for anything in the world want to lose his cook and overseer and duly dissuaded the penitent from her design, calling it an idle fancy inspired by the devil to disturb the serenity of her soul.

No, her place was in this world, and there she would have to remain for the edification of the parishioners. Were there not nuns who had damned themselves for the sin of missing their vocation? Now there was a profound thought for her to meditate on.

Marie Calumet meditated so well on this profound thought that by that very evening she had dismissed all the convents and all the nuns of the universe from her mind.

Her confessor had told her so, hadn't he? There was nothing else for her to do, was there?

But never, never would the unfortunate maiden forget the blow to her innocence. She would suffer so much shame here on earth that good old Saint Peter would not have to keep the door to Paradise shut very long when her time came.

But this obsession must be chased from her mind at any price, or...

One evening, when we were nearing the end of September, Marie Calumet, her voluminous person hidden by the shade of the lamp, decided to discuss the problem with her curé, who was in the dining room.

She came straight to the point. ''M'sieu le curé, I'm going away.''

The priest sat up with a start.

She was going away! The word alone held a future fraught with peril. She would leave him, abandon him, she who had brought him such happiness, who had rebuilt his rectory on a foundation as solid as a rock? Unthinkable!

''You're leaving, Marie? Entering a convent? But haven't I told you...''

''Not for long, M'sieu le curé.''

The curé breathed easier.

''Oh, so you're paying a little visit to Sainte

Geneviève?"

"Forgive me, M'sieu le curé, but I'm going to have my picture took."

"You're having yourself photographed? Where?"

"In Mo'real, M'sieu le curé."

At last, Marie Calumet spoke of her wish to pass her likeness on to posterity by means of photography. She confessed that this fancy had grown to be an obsession which had plagued her for the last two weeks, and that it was the cause of her strange behavior which surely no one had failed to notice, shameful blunders, some of which she dared not specify, and which she deplored with all the sincerity of perfect contrition.

"You understand, I hope," objected Monsieur le curé, "that I can't let you go for long. I have put all my affairs into your hands and I am certain that everything would fall apart if you were to be gone too long. I have things under control now and I am much too pleased to let them revert to their former state."

"No, no, M'sieu le curé, I wouldn't think of spending even one night away from the rectory. I tell you, as truly as you're sitting there, that I'll just take the time to get myself photographed, see a bit of the city, and come right back. So you can see," she concluded, smoothing her hair with the palm of her plump hand, "that I won't be gone for long."

"May God grant it. But you never know..."

"Uncle, uncle!" Suzon burst into the room, quite out of breath.

"Well, what is it?" asked the curé.

"The cat's tumbled into the milk pail!"

"Then fish her out and give the milk to the pigs."

"To the pigs!" protested the niece with one of her delicious pouts. "How could you, uncle! We can't be wasting our milk!"

"Will you listen to this child?" Marie Calumet raised her arms in indignation. "You can't be serious, Suzon! Expecting Monsieur le curé to drink that disgusting slop, where the dratted cat has dragged her behind for the past half hour? Certainly we have to economize, but there are limits! We'll have to give the milk to the little squeakers. We have to have a little cleanliness around here, goodness gracious!"

Dripping milk on the potted plants, her fur bristling like a porcupine's, the cat appeared in the doorway, meowing mournfully.

"Get out, you disgusting thing!" shouted the housekeeper and, with her slipper, administered a well-aimed kick to the animal.

"When are you leaving?" inquired the curé, rising from the table.

"Tomorrow morning."

"You're going away?" the nosy Suzon immediately had to know.

"Going to have my picture took."

"Where?"

"In Mo'real."

"Take me with you!"

"You are needed here," the curé intervened peremptorily.

Suzon left without another word.

Our friend now busied herself with the preparations for tomorrow's long voyage until the hour was very late.

From her dresser, she took her beautiful black wool skirt with the flounce, her shawl with its brilliant patterns, woolen stockings she herself had knitted which reached halfway up her thighs, her pantaloons and petticoat of yellow cotton trimmed with narrow red wool lace, her camisole which rose chastely to her chin, her outsized straw hat that was adorned with an orchard, her gloves, and her cloth boots with elastic straps, not to mention her cross on its chain.

For such contingencies as shopping and carrying a few little snacks — you can never tell what might happen — the traveler reached under her spindle bed and brought out her carpetbag. It would be no exaggeration to say that this piece of luggage was as large as a haversack.

When she had finished, the good woman undressed, said her prayers, and stretched out on her woolen country sheets. Dipping her fingers into the white stone holy-water basin suspended at the head of her bed, she made the Sign of the Cross, gave her heart to the Lord, and went to sleep.

In the morning, she rose with the crow of the rooster. Her ablutions, of necessity, had to be more thorough than on ordinary days. The train was due at Saint Ildefonse at seven-fifteen. The station was located at least five miles from the rectory, a distance Marie could not cover on foot.

The curé, therefore, had given orders for his hired man to bring the spanking new buggy, bought barely two weeks ago, from the coach house and to harness the gray mare.

The mare, her eighteen years notwithstanding, was not a bad animal, though she was beginning to feel a bit of rheumatism in her legs.

It was not an order, but a special privilege Monsieur le curé was giving Narcisse, and never had the hired man obliged with more promptness and pleasure.

He had polished the buggy until it shone like a mirror and had curried the mare so thoroughly that not an atom of dung or dust remained on her gray coat.

Moreover, and this is something he had never done

for anyone, not even Monsieur le curé, he had decorated Rosinante's ears with poppy-red ribbons.

The housekeeper was ready, her carriage waiting.

Narcisse had not yet arrived.

"Narcisse!" Monsieur le curé, Marie Calumet, and Suzon took turns in calling. "Hurry, Narcisse!"

Our traveler was on pins and needles. What if she missed her train? Ah, here was Narcisse at last, wearing his Sunday best!

It was the first time that he had the good fortune to accompany the light of his life, the apple of his eye, the ruler of his soul. In order to please her a little bit, he had wanted to be as handsome, as irresistible as possible, though alas, he had little faith in the power of his charms.

It was one of those mornings full of freshness and sun, when it feels good to be alive.

To the irregular trot of the mare, Monsieur le curé's buggy set off amid two hedges of grain which would soon be harvested, its fruit falling into the fields like golden rain.

Along the sides of the road, wild cherry trees, poplars, willows, and mountain ash stand alined like soldiers in review. Thrushes and swallows and blackbirds roosting on fences or trees salute the carriage's passage with their merry chirping.

"Good morning, Marie Calumet!"

"Have a good trip, Marie Calumet!"

"Come back soon, Marie Calumet!"

The housekeeper is filled with childish joy. Greedily, she breathes in the fragrance of this rural perfume.

Narcisse is paralyzed with amorous fear, his tongue glued to his palate. The only words he utters from time to time, mechanically, while his mind is elsewhere, are orders to the mare. "Giddy up, Gray! Hoi, old Gray!

Get a move on!"

And again he sinks into the depths of reverie.

"How beautiful she is," he muses.

The woman who brushes so closely against him reminds him of a succulent apple whose brilliant red skin, contrasting with its trembling green leaves, invites the beholder to devour it with relish.

Twenty times, seeing her so beguilingly attired and sensing her mellow mood, he thought of risking another declaration of his ardor. And twenty times, the withering memory of her last rebuff sealed his lips hermetically.

A strident and prolonged whistle caused the mare to perk up her ears and to quicken her pace.

The train was pulling into the station.

"Hurry!" said Marie Calumet, alarmed.

Fortunately the buggy was only a few hundred yards from the station — a pompous word for a rabbit hutch which stank of grease and filth.

When the carriage came to a halt, Monsieur le curé's housekeeper leapt, rather than stepped, from the vehicle and burst into the station like a whirlwind.

"My ticket! My ticket! Quickly, for the love of God!"

"Where is it you're going?" inquired the railway employee, who occupied the triple position of telegraph operator, ticket seller, and handyman.

"Where is it I'm going! To Mo'real, of course!"

"Now that's a good one," she thought. "Doesn't everyone know that I'm going to Mo'real?"

"First or second?"

"What?"

"Do you want a first-class ticket or a second-class ticket? That's not too difficult for you, is it?"

"Does it cost less in second class?"

"Of course."

"Sell me a second class, then."

Lined up behind her, four or five farmers, bound for Petite Misère, La Déchirure, La Vesse Bleue, and Vide Poche, were waiting for the same train.

They were frantic with impatience.

The train snorted.

His indisputable gallantry notwithstanding, Narcisse had not been able to reach the curé's housekeeper in time to assist her with her ticket negotiations.

He was, nevertheless, determined to play every last one of his trump cards and, throwing himself into the pursuit of the city-bound country lass, came to her aid as she boarded the train. Nor did he forget to hand her the carpetbag.

Five minutes later, the convoy began to move.

When it had become a mere black dot in the distance, Narcisse returned to his buggy, wiping away a tear with the back of his hand. How it had come to be there he had no idea.

Chapter XVII

Marie Calumet Goes to Montreal to Have Her Picture Taken

As has been seen, our traveler had bought a second-class ticket. Once on the train, she found that the coach was packed.

In a corner, a churlish farmer, with a pumpkin under one arm and a basket of tomatoes under the other, was squeezed tightly against a peasant woman.

A group of drunken rustics were passing around a bottle of gin, from which they were quenching their thirst, to resounding guffaws and inane, if ribald, jokes.

Holding on to her carpetbag, Marie Calumet stood, nauseated by the rancid emanations of sweat and grease rising from all this human flesh, and grumbled about "those ignoramuses who aren't even well enough educated to give their seat to a lady."

The conductor appeared at the end of the coach. "Tickets! Tickets!" he demanded.

He looked like a stuffed doll with his yellow buttons, broad brick-red face, and John Bull mustache.

It was the first time that Marie Calumet had transported her person on a railway. The only prior voyage in her life had been the one to move her Penates from Sainte Geneviève to Saint Ildefonse. She was completely out of her element.

Observing the other passengers, she plunged her hand into her bag in search of her ticket. She searched and searched.

The conductor, who disliked waiting, fumed in an idiom which was mercifully foreign to Marie Calumet's ears.

"Now where's that darn ticket," she wondered nervously. "I put it into my reticule and that's for sure!"

At last she found it.

The conductor, beneath his rough exterior, turned out not to be a bad fellow after all, for he allowed Marie Calumet to slip into first class.

Instead of nasty wooden benches, she now found herself amid well-sprung red velvet seats. Say what you will, she thought, there were none more beautiful, not even those in the parlor of the rectory.

She fell into her seat, exhausted.

"Aaaah," she sighed happily.

Under the avalanche of the housekeeper's weight, an old maid, dry and yellow as a herring, gathered her freshly ironed pink muslin dress about her, an ill-concealed challenge in her grimace.

"I beg your pardon," said Marie Calumet, quite intimidated, and crossed her hands over her breast.

"It's nothing," answered the old maid, venturing a smile that brought to mind the oral cavity of a marmoset. She retreated further into her corner.

"Lovely day, ain't it, Mamzelle?" noted the housekeeper.

"Yes, Madame."

"Are you going far today?"

"Yes."

Obviously, she was getting nowhere. Shocked by

such unaccustomed coldness, Marie Calumet turned away disdainfully.

On the bench next to hers a pair of newlyweds sat cooing tenderly. The groom wore a frock coat of shiny serge, a boutonniere of artificial flowers in his buttonhole. His skull was crowned by an imposing top hat. The bride was dressed in a badly cut apple-green silk gown, set off by white filet-lace gloves and cream-colored satin shoes.

The rest of the world had ceased to exist for those two lovebirds, on the threshold of their honeymoon.

The woman had lovingly laid her head upon her dear husband's shoulder, and from time to time their fingers irresistibly intertwined with growing excitement.

Further down, faces and hands gummed up by a candy cane, two little monsters clambered onto the knee of a dandy without a trace of shyness. Though extremely ill at ease, the dandy dared not open his mouth, for the monsters' mother had turtle-dove eyes and a chignon that invited kisses.

Four seats behind, an elderly pot-bellied priest was reading his breviary, his glasses perched on a flat nose.

Near one of the doors, a young girl, who looked to be a boarding-school inmate on her way back to the convent, was exchanging furtive glances with a young man whose upper lip was shaded by a hint of hairy growth.

And the train chugged on through olive-green and deep-gold fields, browsing flocks of sheep, herds of cows, and horses that took off in great haste, neighing and kicking, frightened by the passage of the train.

Marie Calumet, who had not eaten a morsel since the previous day, now felt hunger pangs gnawing at the pit of her stomach.

She opened her travel bag and spread a large printed

handkerchief on her knees.

There appeared successively a loaf of homemade bread, a piece of smoked ham, a little jar of plum jam, a wedge of mellow cheese, molasses cookies, a bottle of milk, a knife with a wooden handle, and a pewter spoon.

These elaborate preparations for her snack did not fail to provoke the curiosity and mirth of her fellow travelers. Some even went so far as to utter wounding remarks in a loud voice.

"Hey, little mother," cried one jester, "what happened to the soup?"

"You won't forget to invite me when you get to the dessert, will you?" added a traveling salesman, grinning from ear to ear.

"Careful, lady, or you'll spill your milk!"

And so, to the end of the meal, biting, nasty remarks assailed the housekeeper from every direction.

But Marie Calumet, intelligent woman that she was, pretended not to hear any of them. When she had had her fill, she returned the leftovers to her carpetbag and wiped her mouth and fingers with the kerchief that had served her as a tablecloth.

The train was about to pull into the station. The newlyweds untangled their hands and feet; the sweet darlings relinquished the knees of the elegant Brummel who, as a reward for his forbearance, received a pleasant smile from their mother; the schoolboy rose and furtively slipped a tender note he had just scribbled to the blushing schoolgirl.

Feeling ill at ease when she had stepped from the train, Marie Calumet paused for a few minutes and sniffed the air. Instantly, she was assailed by a host of coachmen who, whips in hand, shouted into her ears, "Carriage, Madam? Barouche, Madam?"

But our traveler never lost sight of the fact that she must not incur unnecessary expenses. Blindly, she elbowed through the crowd until she had threaded her way out of all this confusion.

But where to go now?

She did not know. She had come from her village "to have her picture took in Mo'real." Now, in this strange city, she would have to find a photographer's place of business. Unfortunately, in 1860, photographers weren't to be found on every street corner, and Marie Calumet was forced to go on a voyage of exploration.

She walked down Saint Joseph Street, crossed McGill, continued on Notre Dame, and came to Saint Laurent with its beautiful homes and vast vegetable plots and orchards. When she finally reached Sainte Catherine Street, she was exhausted. A green blanket of countryside stretched before her eyes, dotted with a few modest homes which seemed to have grown up in the shelter of large trees.

It had rained all night and after crossing so many streets, our friend's feet were already caked with mud. And still she had not found her photographer. Yet find him she must, come what may.

A bare-legged little boy, hands buried in the pockets of his pants strolled past. She called out to him, "Say, my boy, could you tell me where I can find a picture-taker in these parts?"

"What for?" asked the little rogue, inserting a finger in his nose.

"To have myself photographed, what else? I haven't come to see a picture-taker to buy aspidistras, you know. Well? Can you tell me?"

"Well, now. If it's to get yourself snapped," he said, pointing the way with his finger, "go straight ahead, walk down Saint Laurent, take Notre Dame Street, turn left at the corner, keep going three or four blocks until you see a large red teakettle. That's where it is. The photographer's on the top floor.''

Marie Calumet opened her eyes wide, accenting every direction with a nod of her head.

"Thanks a lot, my boy."

The little boy went his way.

"Hey!" she shouted, opening her carpetbag, which she had placed on the uneven planks of the sidewalk. She retrieved an enormous apple from the dephts of her bag and, with a smile, offered it to the child. "That's for your trouble."

Crossing the street, the careless woman failed to notice that a streetcar was bearing down on her.

"Careful, lady," shouted the boy, "or you'll get yourself knocked down!"

A curious spectacle now offered itself to Marie Calumet's innocent eyes. Two nags — snotty, eyes watering, tongues hanging out, skeletons clearly outlined, coats threadbare from too many whiplashes, and barely able to maintain their equilibrium — warned pedestrians of their approach with bells attached to their scrawny necks. Behind them, the wretched creatures were pulling something resembling a movable hovel on uneven rails.

Despite her firm resolve not to incur unnecessary expenses, our villager could not resist the temptation to treat herself to the luxury of a streetcar ride.

Before she had time to sit down, the conductor gave a signal with his bell and the animals resumed their indifferent trot, causing Marie to trip and stumble over a black-clad reverend whose knees were as pointed as the teeth of a rake. She mumbled apologies.

The minister growled between his long, flat teeth.

130

"Shocking!"

"Notre Dame!" thundered the conductor.

Marie Calumet leapt to her feet and rushed out, treading on the toes of the other passengers and jostling them with her carpetbag.

Oh! The stream of invective that followed her!

Luckily, she was too preoccupied to notice it and walked quickly towards the red teakettle. Inside, she mounted a dingy, steep staircase, being careful on each step not to break her neck. The upstairs door was open. She entered.

A squinty-eyed young man, with a few hairs under his nose, came traipsing towards her on stork's legs.

"Is this where you can get your picture took?" asked the priest's housekeeper, inspecting the establishment.

"Yes, Madame. Would you like them on zinc or cardboard?"

"Oh, I don't know. It doesn't matter. So long as they look like me and don't cost too much."

"On zinc they will cost you thirty cents for three."

"And on cardboard?"

"Four dollars per dozen."

"I'll take zinc."

It was noon. The young gentleman had not yet had his lunch, and seemed impatient.

"Sit down here, please."

"Hereabouts?"

"Yes, yes, here."

Our rustic heroine would have liked to check her appearance in a mirror, but, seeing none, she dared not ask if she could do so elsewhere in the studio.

Still, she ventured a timid query. "Do I look all right like this, my dear sir?"

"Very good, Madame, very good."

Draping her shawl just so, and adjusting her bonnet just so, he made her turn her head this way and that and lifted up her chin.

"Ready! Pay attention now… no, don't be so serious… you look too severe… smile a little… think of something nice… of someone you love…" Marie Calumet thought of her curé. "Good… good… that's very good. Don't move now… Attention! One… two… attention… three! There you are!"

Marie Calumet would not have moved for the world. So much so that when the photographer said "There you are!" she remained motionless in her seat.

"You may get up now, Madame. It's all over."

While she was waiting for her portraits, the servant mused, "One for Monsieur le curé… one for me… but who'll I give the third one to? Never mind, I'll keep it in reserve, just in case."

A quarter of an hour later, our villager at last took possession of her photographs.

"Gracious Sainte Anne! They look like me!" she exclaimed with delight. "You'd think it's me!"

And having taken a good long look at her portraits, she placed them carefully into her bag.

She payed and walked towards the exit.

"Good-by, M'sieu!"

"Good-by, Madame."

It annoyed Marie Calumet a little that people insisted on calling her "madame" rather than "mademoiselle." Why? Was she that old already? In Saint Ildefonse no one ever made that mistake. But then, she was a celebrity in Saint Ildefonse. Was she aware of that?

The young man, with condescension worth noting, accompanied Monsieur le curé's housekeeper towards the door.

It had been rather cool in the morning, but the temperature had risen now and the sun stood at its zenith. Under the weight of her gaudy cashmere shawl and her carpetbag, our traveler began to sweat profusely.

Where to go now? She still had two hours left. Strolling hither and thither, she came down to Place Jacques Cartier, where she saw a group of farmers displaying their wares, continued to Saint Paul to take a look at its wholesale stores, and turned onto the Commissionaires Street with its public houses, passing in front of the Cassepel Hotel where a person could eat all he wanted for two pennies.

The housekeeper returned via Saint Jean Baptiste Street, pausing in front of the church of Notre Dame de Pitié, and finally found herself under the red teakettle once more. Her poor aching feet nothwithstanding, she marched on toward Notre Dame Street which boasted private homes and a host of strollers. She wanted to take another look at Sainte Catherine Street.

A large number of signs caught her attention: a bare-fanged, grimacing lion held in place by an iron chain around his body; a wide-open scarlet umbrella, large as an awning; a pair of Indian boots, suspended from a long pole; gigantic scissors threatening to extinguish the life of man with one blow; a globe of colossal proportions; and God knows what else. Each of these signs was suspended like a treacherous sword of Damocles over the heads of the passers-by.

The sound of a horn and a cry of alarm, repeated over and over again, assailed her ears. ''Fire! Fire!'' Five minutes later she saw the pump drawn by two firemen, followed in turn by seven or eight galloping firemen and a horde of curious bystanders, all wading through the mud.

Marie Calumet continued on her way, coming to an abrupt halt in front of a novelty store. A strange sight had caught her fancy.

Let the reader imagine an inordinately large bell, measuring over three feet in diameter — a bouffant petticoat spread open, not unlike an umbrella, by metal struts. She approached the window and slowly read the large print of the sign:

BALLOON FOR SALE!
EXCELLENT BARGAIN!

"What could this balloon be for," thought Marie Calumet.

She reflected for a moment.

"It's true," she thought, "it looks like the skeleton of a petticoat, but is there a creature under the sun so profligate as to dress up in such an invention?"

She was determined to satisfy her curiosity and marched boldly into the store.

"Good day, Mamzelle."

"Good day, Madame," answered a young girl, coming towards her.

" 'Mamzelle', if you please," corrected Marie Calumet with a trace of annoyance.

"I beg your pardon, Mamzelle."

"Can you tell me what that thing is for, the one you have in the window?" She pointed towards the strange object.

"This, Madame — sorry, Mademoiselle — is a crinoline, generally known as a balloon."

"Ah bah!"

"Just a minute, I'll show you one just like it."

"Don't bother."

"Oh, it's no bother... Here you are. Would you like to put down your valise by the counter?" While Marie

Calumet bent down to do so, the young girl winked at the other clerks. "It's the big fashion of the day! The very latest! All our well-dressed ladies are mad about it."

"Oh, sure. You'll never make me believe..."

"Oh yes! The spherical form the balloon gives to a dress is so becoming, so pretty! It accentuates the suppleness of the waist and rounds out the hips, which gives them that lovely molded look!

"I'm convinced that a balloon would be perfect for your kind of beauty, Mademoiselle."

"You would say that," said Marie Calumet. "Let her tempt me," she thought.

"I assure you..."

"And how do you wear this balloon?"

"It's very simple — just like a petticoat. But," she added, whispering into the housekeeper's ear, "you must never forget to wear your bloomers, because... after all... you understand... you can never tell..."

"Mamzelle!" Marie Calumet was indignant. "I never, ever forget to wear my bloomers!"

"I believe you, Mademoiselle," the young clerk hastened to answer in conciliatory tones.

"But I can't take it home like this, under my arm, can I?"

"It's easy to carry!" In two movements, the young girl transformed the balloon into a roll.

"May I wrap it for you? It fits you perfectly!"

"How much does it cost?"

"I can let you have it for three dollars."

"Oh, that's too expensive. I'll give you two."

"No, two and a half. Special for you."

"Two."

"Two and a quarter."

"Two."

"All right, then."

The balloon, alas, was worth only a dollar fifty.

The purchaser paid and was on her way. She already regretted her two dollars and was not pleased with her acquisition. Her eccentricity, moreover, would bring her bad luck, as the reader shall see.

There was just enough time left to return to the station. Overcome with fatigue, Marie Calumet hailed a coachman.

Night had already fallen when the train came to a halt in Saint Ildefonse. Narcisse was waiting, accompanied by Zéphirin. Monsieur le curé had not judged it proper to let his housekeeper and hired man come home alone in the dark.

"Well then, Mamzelle!" asked Narcisse as he helped her into the carriage, "and how did you like the big city of Mo'real?"

"Don't even talk to me about it, because I didn't see any of it. The houses were hiding it all. Imagine, when I got off the train, there was this bunch of coachmen…"

Chapter XVIII

Now You See It, Now You Don't!

The grain had been harvested. Granaries were groaning under the wealth brought in from the fields, and to celebrate the general prosperity, the farmers had organized a festival to which the entire parish had been invited. For a long time to come, the people of Saint Ildefonse, and even those living as far as ten miles away, were to remember the event, which coincided happily with the return of Marie Calumet from Montreal.

One perceptive fellow even stated that the main cause for all this rejoicing on that day was the fact that Monsieur le curé's housekeeper had returned safely from the myriad perils of a visit to the city.

Naturally Monsieur le curé, being the most important member of the parish, had been invited, and he had accepted the invitation eagerly. Moreover, he had given Narcisse orders to harness the gray mare and go to Saint Apollinaire to ask Curé Lefranc if he would honor them with his presence.

Curé Flavel's friend — good neighbors being good friends — did not hesitate for a second. His assistant would replace him during his absence.

The festivities took place at the foot of Saint

Ildefonse's hillock, which, on that day, seemed to have adorned itself with its most brilliant finery.

All morning long there was an uninterrupted coming and going of carts transporting villagers and refreshments. They came in groups of twelve, even fifteen, traveling the road to pleasure piled up in the large hay wagons.

Gradually, the traffic thinned out. The horses were unharnessed, and each was given a fork of hay.

From a distance, the scene was reminiscent of a medieval battlefield. Men, women, children, beasts, and wagons all seemed blended into one confusing tableau.

As befitted their rank, Messieurs les curés Flavel and Lefranc were the last to arrive.

The curé's niece was a picture of loveliness in a white muslin dress, held in at her waist by a magenta ribbon.

The child was chattering without rhyme or reason. She was overflowing with mad gaiety. The mere thought of attending the joyous festivities at her boyfriend's side caused her nearly to burst with happiness. It was easy to tell that she was counting on experiencing delights and mysteries as yet unknown to her.

Narcisse, on the other hand, his hair all glossy but for a kiss-curl in the center of his forehead, looked gloomy. He seemed to have a premonition of imminent misfortune, even disaster.

In the warmth of this September day, the bells over by the turn of the road suddenly rang out the noontime Angelus and drowned out all the voices and shouts.

The villagers, whose faith was at once childlike and strong as the sap of the oak, obeyed the instincts of a habit as old as their soil and, abruptly abandoning their games and laughter, removed their hats. As the steely notes rose into the azure sky, the curé began: *"Angelus Domini nuntiavit Mariae."*

And the village answered in unison: *"Et concepit de Spirituo sancto."*

To the accompaniment of the bell, the prayer, uttered in profound piety, rose towards the Eternal.

Then the games and shouts resumed.

Ten minutes later Zéphirin, who had been detained by his duties as verger, appeared on the field.

More cross-eyed than ever, he wore a heavy gilded copper watch-chain, which dangled across his belly.

Narcisse was standing apart from the others. He had not yet said a word. Finally, he approached Curé Flavel.

"M'sieu le curé," he said, "Mamzelle Marie isn't here. Would you perhaps know where she could be?"

"Marie Calumet not here... Well, I'll be!"

The question passed from mouth to mouth. Presently everyone wondered with growing anxiety, "What's happened to Marie Calumet?"

Marie Calumet and the festivities were one and the same thing. It followed that if there was no Marie Calumet, there could be no festivities.

Had something bad happened to her? Some accident perhaps? Oh no! It was unthinkable, it would be such a pity!

"I saw her half an hour before I left," noted Curé Flavel.

"And me, a quarter of an hour," added Suzon.

"When I passed by the rectory on my way here," said Zéphirin, with a malicious glance at Narcisse, "she was wearing her underpinnings and waved hello to me."

"Don't listen to him!" intervened Monsieur le

curé's hired man, "It's just one of his stories."

"And what do you know, you old…"

"Here, here, none of that nonsense," thundered Monsieur le curé, separating the two rivals.

But the tongues would not stop wagging. How was it possible? Marie Calumet was late? Marie Calumet who was promptitude personified? Why had she not come when all the others did?

If only Narcisse were missing too, at least they could have conjectured…

But no, no! This was Marie Calumet, after all, a wholesome girl who served as an example to the entire county.

Women like Marie Calumet are above suspicion.

Perhaps she was merely not well?

In any case, there would be news of her soon, as Narcisse resolutely — and with what determined strides — returned to the rectory.

He had just reached the end of the field when Marie Calumet appeared in a cloud of dust. The cart came to a halt.

General hilarity broke out.

How about that! This? Marie Calumet? Impossible! Yet there was no mistake!

Was this barrel, this monumental goat-skin bottle, Marie Calumet?

The entire crowd was enraptured.

When I say, "entire crowd," I exaggerate. Monsieur le curé was livid with rage. And as for his hired man — Narcisse was overcome with searing sorrow.

This delirious mob was making fun of Marie Calumet, of the woman whom, in spite of everything, he stubbornly looked on as his betrothed. Oh, the scoundrels! How he wished to see all their heads fused into one that he might sever it with one blow, emulating the Roman emperor who, centuries before Narcisse, had longed to commit this same act.

On the other hand, the unfortunate man could sense that people had good cause to deride Marie Calumet, and this awareness saddened him all the more.

How could a lass as intelligent as Marie Calumet do a thing like this?

That was the question Narcisse kept asking himself.

For the first display of her crinoline, Monsieur le curé's housekeeper had decided to wait for a special occasion, for a feast at which the entire village of Saint Ildefonse would be gathered.

She could not have chosen a better occasion.

She had wanted to create a sensation.

Her wish, alas, was granted only too well!

Before she began to dress, the rectory servant had seen to it that everyone else had gone ahead to join the festivities.

And therein lies the explanation of her tardiness, which had strangely escaped the rectory household in their excitement. For the housekeeper had, in fact, told them not to wait for her, having been delayed, as she had explained, by important business. She had told them not to worry, that she would join them shortly, that she would somehow find herself a ride.

When it came to donning her balloon which she had kept hidden under her bed, she had a moment's trepidation. What if this latest article of fashion were to cause a scandal?

What would Monsieur le curé say?

She would be driven from the rectory in shame, of that there was not the shadow of a doubt.

Should she brave public opinion? In Montreal, she had been told that all elegant ladies wore this kind of crinoline. She should have consulted Monsieur le curé and Suzon as, by the way, she did every time she bought the most innocuous article at the village's general store.

The more she looked into the mirror, the more enormous she found herself.

Her resolve faltered, but, in the end, eccentricity won out. It was to be her downfall.

She stepped into her crinoline, added a blouse with a heart-shaped neckline, and remembered to wear the little silver cross suspended on a narrow black velvet ribbon.

In this outlandish get-up, she surveyed herself one last time and went down the stairs, catching on every piece of furniture.

The blacksmith, who had had several horses to shoe, had been late starting for the party. Now, with his brood in his barouche, he was on his way when he saw, a hundred yards ahead of him, something which reminded him of a ship pitching and rolling in distress.

"Hey, old woman," he said to his wife, "you've got good eyes. "What's that over there?"

"It sure looks like a creature to me, but I can't say for certain."

The blacksmith cracked his whip and soon they pulled up beside the strange apparition.

"It's Mamzelle Marie Calumet, if I'm not mistaken!"

"Marie Calumet!"

"Hey, will you take a look at Marie Calumet!"

"Holy cow!"

"You've suddenly put on a lot of weight!"

"What's that you're carrying under your skirt?"

Every member of the family had to put in his penny's worth.

Several times, the housekeeper opened her mouth to proffer an explanation. It proved futile.

"Well, get in, get in!" said the blacksmith. "You can tell us all about it on the way."

Get in, eh? That was easier said than done. There was room for Marie Calumet all right. But for her balloon?

When it turned out to be impossible, Gustave gallantly gave up his seat. He would walk.

To make up for lost time, the blacksmith took off at full gallop. It was in the cloud of dust raised by his barouche that the villagers were treated to their first sight of Marie Calumet and her crinoline.

When at last she stepped down, or rather was hauled off the barouche, Marie Calumet looked stunned. Being the object of so many malicious pleasantries caused her to lose her composure.

That's what you get for wanting to introduce the latest fashion to Saint Ildefonse, especially this kind of fashion.

It was getting late, however, and the curé's housekeeper, renowned as the most accomplished cook in the village, was asked to preside over the preparations for the feast.

The gallant Narcisse eagerly went this way and that, doing the work of four. He gathered rocks and laid them out in circles two feet high, filling the interior with birch-bark kindling. On these stone hearths, he placed pot-bellied cast-iron vessels. Finally, he lit a match, and soon the flames were crackling joyously.

The cook pushed up her sleeves, tied on an apron, and busied herself, heating the soup — a pea soup which she had enriched with slices of lard and seasoned with parsley.

Despite her crinoline, which hampered her movements severely, our cordon bleu cook labored assiduously.

Noting that she was tiring herself out, Curé Flavel told her to rest for a spell.

Without interrupting her work, Marie Calumet turned to answer him, and did so at her cost — she failed to see the root of a walnut tree underfoot.

And there occurred that deplorable accident which the salesgirl in the novelty store had tried to prevent with some wise counsel.

The unfortunate lass tripped on the root and fell flat on her back.

The balloon, decidedly, was not a good invention.

An ordinary petticoat could always be counted on to adapt to the occasional delicate situation, but with this article, fashioned with thin strips of bone or metal, it was a different story altogether.

And to make the tragedy complete, the housekeeper, who had so indignantly declared that she always wore her bloomers, had, in her haste, forgotten to step into that vital garment.

Seeing for the first time what he had never seen before, the chaste Curé Flavel blushed like a poppy. He made the Sign of the Cross.

Curé Lefranc risked an eye and choked. It was imperative to maintain decorum. Imperative!

Suzon was bursting with laughter, and Zéphirin could not feast his eyes enough.

But Narcisse, who remembered hearing, at the village school, an Old Testament story about a mishap which befell Noah in his cups, rushed to the aid of his friend. He did so, let it be noted, walking backwards.

Chastely, he averted his eyes.

Her cheeks afire, in superb anger, Marie Calumet now lashed out with a searing reproach. ''You're nothing but a bunch of pigs!"

Tears came to her eyes, and she pointed to Narcisse. "Here at least is a man who, instead of acting like a bunch of stupid toads, has the gumption to defend a poor girl in distress. Your arm, M'sieu Narcisse."

Silence.

And a large, swaying bell could be seen receding into the distance amid a swirl of dust turned to gold by the oblique rays of the sun.

When Marie Calumet had gone, enjoyment was no longer possible. Already, the festive mood was shattered and there was talk of going home.

Monsieur le curé climbed on a cart. "My dear friends," he began, "you have just witnessed a truly scandalous occurrence. I, for my part, would like to believe that there was no wicked intention on the part of my housekeeper. As for me, I swear to you that I knew absolutely nothing of the whole affair. Here you have, my dear brothers, a shocking example of the shameless fashions in the large cities. Now listen to me carefully, my dear sisters. I forbid you to wear these revolting petticoats, these balloons. And if ever one of you should decide to disobey me, let her be exposed to ridicule and public scorn and be excluded from my church."

The severe words uttered by the man of God added a final chill, and the festivities ended forthwith.

Back at the rectory, the housekeeper went to her room. She wriggled out of her crinoline and trampled it with rage.

Not satisfied with this act of vandalism, she carried it to the stove. There she made a roaring fire to insure that nothing would remain of the confounded invention.

Chapter XIX

At Last!

During the night which followed that memorable day, Narcisse had dreams of shocking lubricity. To avoid verbosity, I shall simply inform the reader that our suitor dreamt that he was married.

The dream, if it was a dream, had the effect of bringing down a rain of salutary comfort on his heart, so seared by despair and unrequited love.

As soon as he rose from his bed, he made his decision. On thinking matters over, he believed that circumstances were more propitious now. First of all, he had ingratiated himself with Marie Calumet. Hadn't he? Surely he had, for she had praised him in front of the entire village, and she had asked him to accompany her back to the rectory. And then, this dream! Our Narcisse had a blind faith in dreams, for he was as superstitious as only a countryman can be.

He dressed hurriedly and went downstairs hoping to meet Marie Calumet.

He saw her almost immediately, on her way outside with her little stool and her pails. She was going to milk her cows.

Once again, his blood rushed to his heart.

His voice quavered. "Mamzelle Marie?"

"Narcisse?"

"Mamzelle Marie, I don't know anymore how to tell you this 'cause it's already brought me bad luck but... but... after what you'd told me yesterday... I believe... I believe... Would you permit me to flirt with you..."

"What?"

"I mean, woo..."

"You're sure, Narcisse, you're not just teasing me?"

"On my good conscience before the good Lord, Mamzelle Marie..."

"All right, then! You're a good fellow, Narcisse. You proved it yesterday. Come court me the way it should be done, and if we take to each other, well then, we'll get married!"

"So the other..."

"What other?"

"Zéphirin."

"The verger? I never gave him a thought. Him neither."

"Him! Well, I never! Upon my word, Mamzelle, you may not believe this... but only last week..."

"You can tell me another time. I've got to milk my cows now."

"All right, Mamzelle Marie, I'll tell you the first time I spend an evening with you. Tonight?"

"Tonight? No, not tonight, 'cause I have to scrub my kitchen floor. Tomorrow."

"Tomorrow. Fine. Tomorrow then."

Marie Calumet went off to milk the cows, and Narcisse to tend the pigs and the gray mare of the rectory.

If Marie Calumet did not hesitate to give Narcisse an affirmative answer it was because after the disaster with her balloon, she, too, had made up her mind. And once Marie Calumet, with that resolute temperament of hers, made up her mind, she made up her mind and there were never two ways about that.

She had even said to herself, "Another time, if Narcisse asks me to marry him, it won't take me long. I suit you, you suit me, we're agreed!"

Still, for a bit, she had been worried that her admirer would not ask her again.

And so it was with real satisfaction that she had answered Narcisse: "If we take to each other, we'll get married."

Narcisse, it goes without saying, was delirious. Whenever he met an acquaintance, he would immediately whisper, "I'm getting married, you know."

"You?"

"Oh yes."

"And to whom?"

"What do you mean, to whom? To Marie Calumet, of course!"

"You don't say!"

"Oh yes, but don't tell anyone. You're the only one who knows."

The same conversation took place at every meeting.

For thirty days, Narcisse courted Marie Calumet discretely and faithfully. He came down from his garret at seven o'clock and returned there at ten.

The betrothed spent the evenings in the kitchen, or in the parlor, always sitting in opposite corners, and always in company with the curé or Suzon.

It was a Wednesday evening. The kitchen was lit by a lamp filled to the brim with coal oil. Marie Calumet was washing dishes on a small table next to the sink. Suzon was drying them. Curé Flavel, sitting on a large, cretonne-covered rocking chair, smoked silently, his feet resting on the apron of the stove, which purred more loudly than the cat, who stretched out beside it, her almond-shaped eyes half closed.

An atmosphere of warmth, serenity, and well-being pervaded the room.

Outside, the wind was howling like an amorous tomcat. Rain beat down on the windows in a monotone patter.

With a dry, crackling sound, a spark leapt through the small round opening in the stove and fell to the floor.

And there was silence again.

"That means we're going to have a visitor," remarked Marie Calumet, breaking the silence.

At that precise moment the door opened and Narcisse appeared in a gust of wind and rain.

Seeing him hesitate in the doorway, the curé called, "Close the door, or the house will float away."

"This is dog's weather, if you ask me," answered Narcisse. "It's raining buckets."

Monsieur le curé's hired man looked very serious tonight, so much so that Suzon, who was an observant lass, called out to him, "Hey, Narcisse! You look like the man who swallowed the cat!"

Narcisse said nothing.

He removed his water-logged cap and took a few steps towards Marie Calumet. "Mamzelle Marie, there's no point in fooling around any longer, 'cause you know very well, and M'sieur le curé says it too, that everything that gets dragged out gets soiled."

The housekeeper dropped her dishcloth, Suzon dropped her towel, the curé dropped his pipe.

"Mamzelle Marie, I'm not going to beat about the bush. Do you want me for your man?"

It was clear that Narcisse had done his homework. He was making a supreme effort to speak with such assurance.

"I'm not rich," he added, "but I'm strong and healthy. And that's without counting that I love you a whole lot. The two of us could raise a good Christian family. Isn't that true, father?"

"Right you are, Narcisse."

But Marie Calumet said nothing.

She wiped her clammy hands on her apron.

"Do you want to ? How about it?" repeated Narcisse, fearing the worst.

Marie Calumet acquiesced at last.

"Yes, Narcisse."

She held out her hands to him. "I'll make you a good wife."

And, turning to Curé Flavel, "M'sieu le curé, papa and maman are dead — may God rest their souls in Perpetual Light — will you take their place and give me away to this good fellow?"

Since he could not locate a handkerchief, Monsieur le curé wiped his eyes with the back of his hand.

"Yes. But what will become of me without you?"

"Don't worry, M'sieu le curé. We'll work it all out, you'll see."

"Well, if it has to be, I wish you happiness, my children."

He pushed them towards one another. "Go ahead. Embrace."

Just then the verger entered the room. Maliciously, Suzon said to him, "Zéphirin, let me present M'sieu and Madame Boisvert."

"Oh!" said the astonished verger.

And without adding another word, he walked out the door which opened on the backyard.

Two weeks later, on the eve of the wedding, Monsieur Ménard, the notary, knocked on the door of the rectory.

Being the only notary in the parish, Maître Ménard did not fear competition. He seldom bothered to make calls. Business was generally transacted in his office. But this was not so when it came to Monsieur le curé and Marie Calumet. They deserved respect and that is why he had come to the rectory in person.

When he had inquired about his host's health and offered congratulations to Marie Calumet, the notary produced two large sheets of paper which he folded with his thumb to make a wide margin for endorsements and footnotes.

He cleared his throat, sat down at the priest's desk and began to write while the others, in order not to disturb him, whispered in low voices.

Before Maître Antoine Ménard, notary public for the Province of Quebec, residing and practising in the parish of Saint Ildefonse, have appeared:

Narcisse Boisvert, hired man of Monsieur le curé Flavel, eldest son issued from the marriage between the late Prosper Boisvert, farmer at Pain Sec and the late Dame Caroline Dubuc of the same address, said Narcisse Boisvert acting under his own name, Party of the First Part;

And Demoiselle Marie Calumet, of Sainte Geneviève, eldest daughter issued from the marriage between the late Athanase Calumet, of the same address and the late Dame Sophie Cadotte of Saint Joseph de la Tabatière, the aforementioned Demoiselle Marie Calumet also acting in her own name, Party of the Second Part;

Who have agreed, according to the civil conditions

applying to the marriage planned between them:

That there shall be community of goods between the future spouses...

"Narcisse," asked the notary, peering at the hired man over his glasses, "are you proposing to settle a dowry on your future spouse?"

"Yes, M'sieu le notaire."

"How much?"

"Two hundred dollars."

The notary wrote:

In consideration of the future spouse's affection for his future wife, he is hereby making a donation which is duly accepted by the future spouse.

Firstly: The sum of two hundred dollars, which he undertakes to furnish to the future spouse at any time following the celebration of the marriage, either in a single or several payments, as stipulated by his future spouse.

Should the future spouse decease before the payment of the entire sum or part thereof, it is expressly understood that the future spouse shall be released from the obligation to pay the outstanding amount, the dowry in question becoming null and void at such time.

Secondly...

"Is there a secondly?" inquired the notary.

Narcisse and Marie Calumet said nothing. What was he talking about? They had no idea.

"Yes," answered the curé, "there is a secondly. Write down that in recognition of the services she has performed for me, I wish to make a gift to my house-keeper."

The notary wrote:

In consideration of the gratitude for uncalculable services rendered by the party of the second part to the

Reverend Monsieur Flavel, parish priest at Saint Il-defonse, the said Curé Flavel makes a gift, pure, simple, and irrevocable, and intended to serve her best interests, to the aforementioned Demoiselle Marie Calumet, said gift consisting of:

"What are you giving?" asked the notary, raising his head from the sheet of paper on the desk.

All eyes now turned toward the priest who was smiling with mischief and kindliness. The house-keeper, in particular, could not believe her ears. The curé began, "A dairy cow, which I pledge to replace in case of death."

"M'sieu le curé!" cried Marie Calumet, "that really doesn't make any sense at all!"

The scribe recorded: *One immortal cow.*

"One fair-sized pig," continued the curé.

"M'sieu le curé, you can't be serious!"

A reasonable pig, scribbled the notary.

"One fertile sow."

"M'sieu le curé!"

Ignoring Marie Calumet's exclamations, the notary wrote: *A sow with income.*

"Twelve hens," continued the curé.

"M'sieu le curé, you're ruining yourself!" cried the future bride.

Twelve hens, repeated the scribe.

"Are you pleased, my children?"

"Oh, M'sieu le curé!"

"Is that all?" asked Maître Ménard.

Blushing a little, Narcisse prodded. "Hey, M'sieu le curé, how'd you like to throw in a rooster?"

Suzon, who, thus far, had not been able to get a word in edgewise, burst out laughing.

Marie Calumet showed plainly that she was greatly displeased with her fiancé's audacity.

"A rooster it is!" said the curé, laughing heartily.

Twelve hens of which one a rooster, added the notary.

They discussed a few more clauses before the notary gave the document a complete reading. Then he added in one of the margins:

The above-mentioned parishes of Sainte Geneviève and Saint Apollinaire are one and the same parish, the name of Saint Apollinaire having been given to the former after the birth of Demoiselle Marie Calumet.

He concluded:

After reading the present document, the future spouses and witnesses having assisted in the execution of same, have signed before the undersigned.

(Signed) Marie Calumet
   Narcisse X. Boisvert
   Jacques Flavel, priest
   Suzon Flavel
   Antoine Ménard, N.P.

Narcisse could not write. He drew a cross. The curé signed for him.

The signature of the notary was remarkable for its flourish and illegibility.

Finally, according to custom, the notary embraced the future bride and Monsieur le curé poured some rhubarb wine to toast the happiness of the hero of the day.

Meanwhile, the verger was plotting vengeance. Ever since the night of the proposal, he had spoken to no one. He came into the rectory only to eat and to sleep.

One evening, as he was filling the cruets with sacramental wine, he shouted, "I'll get even with the slob!"

154

Chapter XX

A Verger's Revenge

For the first time since the building of the rectory, the sound of mundane celebrations would shatter the walls of that saintly place.

The world and its frivolities would vitiate the atmosphere of peace and virtue which pervaded its every room.

A wedding feast at the rectory! The words are fraught with ambiguity for they denote an inconsistency which might well be held suspect, had not the event been brought about naturally, by force of circumstance.

We can already hear the murmurs of disapproval.

But let timid consciences rest assured. Nothing occurred which was not compatible with human decency. The prudish would not have been able to detect the slightest irregularity, had it not been for... But these were trifles hardly worth mentioning.

Had it not been so, Curé Flavel would never have consented to the celebration of a village wedding feast in his rectory.

How could he have done otherwise, this man who was kindliness personified? What, after all, could he have done? His housekeeper and his hired man were getting married. They were living under his roof. They had no other home. Should they marry and not have a wedding feast! Impossible! Unthinkable! A marriage ring and a wedding feast are all of one piece. At least that was Curé Flavel's understanding.

Still, Marie Calumet thought it necessary to charge Suzon with the task of probing the worthy man's intentions, and the little imp had thought up a headful of arguments, all of which she considered irrefutable.

The priest was bent over his worktable. Suzon crept up to him on tiptoe and placed her hands over his eyes.

"Is that you, Suzon?"

"Yes, uncle, it's me," she said sweetly.

But before she could launch into her opening plea:

"Say, Suzon, about Marie Calumet's and Narcisse's wedding. It's all very nice, but where will the wedding feast be?"

"That's just what I came to..."

"What I thought is that the good Lord will not hold it against me too much if it were to take place right here, in the rectory."

"Oh, what a wonderful idea, M'sieu le curé," cried Suzon happily, clapping her hands and jumping up and down joyously.

And without waiting to hear him out, she scampered off to announce the good news to Narcisse and Marie Calumet.

There was no time to lose, for the wedding would take place eight days hence. Aided by Narcisse and even by Monsieur le curé himself, the two girls turned the house upside down in an orgy of cleaning.

"Wait 'til you see how clean my rectory is going to be," Marie Calumet said proudly. "It'll look brand spanking new."

The kitchen stove never grew cold. The housekeeper and her little assistant cooked, roasted, baked, grilled, stuffed, larded, eviscerated, braised, glazed, breaded, dressed. In short, who would have believed it? The rectory seemed to have been converted into an inn about to open its doors to an entire regiment.

The villagers outdid each other angling for an invitation.

The rectory had a constant stream of callers, each coming under some pretext but with the secret design of being included on the guest list. Some even went so far as to pay their outstanding tithes.

Escaping from the kitchen in delicious wafts, the smell alone pleasantly tantalized their nostrils. There was, of course, also the honor of being received at Monsieur le curé's table. And last but not least, the very understandable pride in being able to say later, "When I went to Marie Calumet's wedding..." — just as the patriots of 1837 were always saying, "When I was at St. Eustache, at St. Charles, at St. Denis..." Marie Calumet already wore a nimbus of immortality. No living soul, Monsieur le curé excepted, could reach up even to her ankle.

They all wanted to be invited, but, unfortunately, they were not. There were grumblings, of course, but these subsided as time went on. For they all knew that, had the rectory been as large as Curé Flavel's heart, the entire parish would have sat down at the pastoral table.

In the midst of all the feverish activity, the verger did not remain idle. Vengeance! Oh, indeed, he had his heart set on vengeance!

Should he mar the virginal purity of the sheets by piercing with a dagger the breast that no man's hand had yet caressed? Should he splatter the walls with the brains of his rival?

No. That would be too banal. It belonged in cheap

novels in which intrigue begins with a slight pressure of the hand in the perfumed boudoir of a seductive woman.

Assassination was too awkward a game. It would create endless complications. And besides would it really be vengeance? The transition from life to death lasts but an instant. It would all be over too quickly.

"They'll live," he growled, rolling his eyes fiercely, "but they'll pay for it, by golly, by golly. I'll show them, I promise!"

Now, here is how Zéphirin undertook to satisfy his thirst for revenge.

On the morning of the wedding, after the ceremony, he secretly slipped towards that edge of the forest which is defined by the river. He searched for a long time. When he had nearly despaired of finding what he was looking for, he uttered a cry of joy.

From now on, it was all a matter of moments. In a trice he had scratched away the bark and chipped off a few glutinous chips of "Leaden Wood."

When he had done this, he found a dark corner where no one could surprise him, lit a fire, and fetched some water from the river in a pan he had hidden, along with a bottle, in the folds of his jacket.

With the patience of a true evil-doer, he boiled this water and poured it over the "Leaden Wood," which he had placed in the bottle. The resulting solution was a sure-fire laxative.

He corked the bottle, slipped it into his jacket, hid the pan, and returned to the rectory.

Loitering about the kitchen, the verger now lay in wait for the right moment to put his sinister plan into execution.

Marie Calumet and Suzon, summoned by Monsieur le curé, had both left the kitchen.

158

By an extraordinary stroke of luck, not even Narcisse was in the room at the time. (Monsieur le curé's hired man, since his marriage, had been following his wife like a shadow and could be heard murmuring over and over again with naive admiration, "And to think that this woman is mine!")

"Good!" thought Zéphirin, "this is my chance. I had better not muck this up or..."

Carefully, he approached the stove. He had already lifted the lid from the kettle in which pig's-foot stew was simmering when Marie Calumet returned to the kitchen.

Zéphirin blushed and quickly hid the bottle in his large pocket.

"Hello, M'sieu Zéphirin," she said.

The bride had noticed his red face, but she put it down to all the excitement.

"Hello, Mamzelle — pardon me, Madame, I mean. Your stew smells downright delicious."

"Doesn't it, though. You'll be tasting it soon."

"Gee, thanks."

Again Marie Calumet was called into the adjoining room.

This time, Zéphirin did not waste time. He poured the contents of his bottle into the stew and fled to the courtyard, taking care to avoid any untoward encounters.

"And now," he said, "if you think that I'll so much as touch that slop..."

The guests began to arrive at five o'clock.

The first was the mayor, with his saxophone-shaped nose, his yellow hair glued to his temples, his shiny pate, and his lustrous green frockcoat squeezing his stomach. On his arm hung his wife, a pleasingly plump, highly devout woman who divided her time equally between her rosary and her tittle-tattle.

One could then behold, entering in succession: the asthmatic notary, wearing a stiff collar whose tips rose above his ears; the doctor, who never wore suspenders and could not utter a sentence without yanking at his trousers; the churchwardens, all puffed up with dignity; the imposing blacksmith; the storekeeper, who was dry and yellow as parchment and kept saying "you know very well... you know very well...;" the local man of means, who sprayed everyone with spittle when talking; and ever so many others, all accompanied by their wives, who came in round, flat, red, and faded models.

Oh, I nearly forgot the blacksmith's son, Gustave. For the past half hour at least, he could have been found on a sofa that had been pushed to the back of the wall behind the parlor door, in a tête-à-tête with Suzon.

And, as recorded in the fable, what with the opportunity, the tender grass, a lick of the tongue — who knows, perhaps, with the aid of love — the young man could restrain himself no longer. He grabbed Suzon with both hands and kissed her.

"You hurt me," she sighed. But she returned his kiss.

Gustave became heated, daring, and was about to... when Curé Lefranc, who had accepted his friend's invitation, stepped into the room.

He did not see them immediately.

"Now where have I left my breviary, where on earth could it be?" he wondered, searching the room.

He saw the two lovers.

Caught *in flagrante delicto,* the startled Suzon turned red as a pretty pepper.

"Oh, my God!" she exclaimed.

Gustave, looking sheepish, remainded glued to his

160

seat and stared at the floor.

"My children," the intruder remarked casually, "it's a good thing that it was I rather than your own pastor who surprised you in this corner. Otherwise... Now, no indiscretions! Be good!"

And pinching the young girl's chin, he wrenched his eyes from the lace trimming of an undergarment and departed, calling to mind memories of thirty-years' standing.

At long last, the guests were asked to come into the dining room and kindly take their seats.

They did so amid the ear-splitting clatter of chairs, knives, forks, spoons, and plates.

Monsieur le curé was seated at one end of the table. The bride, dressed in a lace-trimmed, puce-colored silk dress, sat on his right; the bridegroom, on his left, suffocating in a tight frockcoat, a garment bequeathed to him by a father less obese than his heir.

Narcisse was beside himself. He was laughing and weeping at the same time.

"Oh, M'sieu le curé," he murmured, leaning toward the pastor. "Oh, M'sieu le curé..."

Marie Calumet was more composed. She kept her eyes lowered modestly. It embarrassed her greatly to be addressed as Madame Narcisse Boisvert.

She was close to believing that it was all a silly dream and that tomorrow she would awaken and be the Marie Calumet she had always been.

And indeed, who would have believed it? To satisfy herself that she was not dreaming, Marie Calumet pinched herself below the knee.

Curé Lefranc presided over the opposite end of the table. If someone had looked under the tablecloth, he would have noticed that he was dining at the kitchen table. The dining-room table had been too small for so many people.

"Where is Zéphirin?" asked Curé Flavel, who had only just noticed the absence of his verger.

"It's true, Zéphirin is missing!" the guests said. "Where could he be?"

"Never mind about him," explained Suzon, serving the cabbage soup. "He's just a jealous fellow who's got what's coming to him."

The explanation seemed natural enough and no one gave the verger another thought.

Zéphirin, as a matter of fact, was crouching behind the vestry, a few yards from the cemetery, and was following the events at the rectory with burning interest.

His revenge must have been dear to him, for he had a healthy fear of the dead. Just to be here, so close to the graves, with his guilty conscience, made his blood run cold. To make matters worse, the weather was freezing, and the wind was howling.

Inside the rectory, however, it was warm and everyone was stuffing himself.

"Let's see, Suzon," said the curé, "what will you give us to eat once we've polished off this cabbage soup?"

As can be seen, Suzon had been promoted to the job of head waitress. She had enlisted the help of two neighbors. Marie Calumet, of course, would have liked to serve the wedding feast herself, but she was given to understand (and not without difficulty) that it would not have been proper.

Suzon, who was taking her role seriously, replied, "Well, M'sieu le curé, apart from what you've already eaten, we have pig's-foot stew with dumplings, tourtières, hot lard, cold lard, a roast of beef, a little

162

suckling pig, beans, blood pudding, buckwheat cakes, stuffed turkey, chicken pies, candies, fritters, blanc-mange, crackers, filbert nuts, biscuits, stewed pumpkin, cream, strawberry jam, apple jelly, sweetmeats, barley coffee, rhubarb wine, gingerbread and a lot of other things too.''

"Listen to her!" Monsieur le curé was proud of his niece. "Doesn't this child have the memory of an elephant?"

Suzon, her cheeks afire, her large black pupils glistening like jade, went from guest to guest with the agility of a doe. As she took Curé Lefranc's soup bowl, she accidentally dropped a knife. She stooped to retrieve it and so did Curé Lefranc. Their hands touched lightly. And again, the priest thought that there was no doubt but that Saint Anthony deserved a great deal of credit.

When the pig's-foot stew with its black sauce, a succulent, appetizing, well-spiced dish, was brought to the table, it was greeted with general rejoicing.

"Am I ever going to eat," said the mayor licking his chops. "It's my favorite dish!"

"Wait 'til you see me!" added the notary. "I am starving!"

"Not half as much as I," remarked the doctor. "Did you make it yourself, Mademoiselle, pardon me, Madame Boisvert?"

"Yes, M'sieu le docteur."

"Then it must be delicious! Right, Monsieur le notaire?"

"Certainly, certainly."

Everyone ate so much that Marie Calumet leaned towards her pastor and whispered in his ear, "If we had gluttons like this every day, we'd soon be out of pocket!"

When the guests had finished their dessert, the mayor, at Monsieur le curé's request, rose to propose a toast to the newlyweds.

The mayor of Saint Ildefonse had a passion for speechmaking. Tonight before supper he had taken Curé Flavel aside and said, "Just a word, M'sieu le curé. I'd like you to ask me to propose a toast to the newlyweds. I'll demur a little, for the sake of convention, but I trust that you'll be kind enough to insist."

And so it was. At the opportune moment, Curé Flavel rose. "Would Monsieur le maire be kind enough to propose a toast to the health of the couple?"

The mayor looked surprised, stricken. "Oh no," he answered, "I couldn't. I really couldn't."

"Come, come now, M'sieu le maire," insisted the curé. "Don't be like that and on this special day, too!"

"Well... if you insist."

He began, "Messieurs les curés, Madame my wife, honored groom and bride, and all here present."

The blacksmith continued to eat. His wife nudged him discretely with her elbow.

"I did not expect, on this exceptionally happy occasion, to... to... to..."

He was unable to continue. He stammered. He blanched. Sweat rose to his brow. A sudden chill ran down his spine, and a dreadful cramp cut his stomach in two.

Everyone called out solicitously. "What's the matter, M'sieu le maire? What's the matter? Are you ill?"

"Ye-es, yes," he had to admit. "For... forgive me..."

And in an effort to maintain a dignity commensurate with his high social position, he left the dining room with measured steps. But no sooner had he crossed the threshold than he broke into a frantic gallop, reaching the "little house" by the shortest possible route.

Still in his hiding place, the verger cackled, "Good! That's number one. The rest will follow soon."

Two minutes later, Marie Calumet came on the run. She tried to open the door of the shack.

"Just a minute please!" groaned a voice from inside.

But let us return to the dining room. The formerly starving notary was making a strange grimace. Under this laboring mask, his nerves were twisting in all directions. Unable to swallow the coffee he had in his mouth, he spat it onto the tablecloth. Next, a sinister crackling could be heard shaking the aging carcass that was Maître Ménard.

"Pfuh!" exclaimed those sitting next to him.

"Oh, M'sieu le notaire!"

"Well, yes. That's the way it is," admitted the afflicted man, rising pitifully. "It happens in the best of families. I guess I had better go home."

He took his hat and went out, his legs spread wide.

"Listen," he said before making his final exit, "you look to me as if you've all been hit. I would advise you not to waste time in breaking this up."

The kitchen door was in constant use.

And in the thick mist of this October day a procession of strange ghosts emerged from the rectory, running, bent over along the fences, near the dairy shed, behind the stable, and even at the bottom of the ditch into which Narcisse had fallen on the morning of his bullfight.

EPILOGUE

With her savings added to those of Narcisse, Marie Calumet bought a small white and green house and a patch of ground scantily sheltered, at this time of year, behind a hedge of thick pines. It stood but a small distance from the rectory.

They were happy.

Nine months after her marriage Madame Narcisse Boisvert gave birth to a little boy with red hair.

Owing to the wise counsel of his housekeeper, to which he often had recourse, Monsieur le curé's affairs — and those of his parish — kept flourishing.

Marie Calumet died at the age of sixty.

The entire village of Saint Ildefonse followed the hearse sadly.

As a crowning gesture to this funeral apotheosis, the villagers donated generously and erected a tomb worthy of the memory of this illustrious woman.